Murder at Dolphin Bay

by

Kathi Daley

This book is a work of fiction. Names, characters, places, and incidents either are products of the author's imagination or are used fictitiously. Any resemblance to actual events or locales or persons, living or dead, is entirely coincidental.

This book is dedicated to the gang at Kathi Daley Books Group Page, who helped me come up with a title for this series. They are listed individually on the next page.

I want to give a shout out to Sergeant Glen Luecke of the Honolulu Police Department for providing information regarding entrance requirements for the HPD. I had to take a few liberties, but Glen's input was invaluable.

I also want to thank the very talented Jessica Fischer for the cover art.

I so appreciate Bruce Curran, who is always ready and willing to answer my cyber questions.

And, of course, thanks to the readers and bloggers in my life, who make doing what I do possible.

Thank you to Randy Ladenheim-Gil for the editing.

Special thanks to Pamela Curran, Vivian Shane, Joanne Kocourek, Taryn Lee, Connie Correll, and Della Williamson for submitting recipes.

And finally I want to thank my sister Christy for always lending an ear and my husband Ken for allowing me time to write by taking care of everything else.

Shelli King
Angie Young
Shirley Fields Layne
Catherine Willson Bogert
Robin Gzikowski Christofaro
Jeannie Dannheim
Donna L. Walo-Clancy
Jan Flynn
Kimberly Perry Gayheart
Martie Peck
Terry Smith
Pam Paison
Sheryl Hagan-Booth
Debra Woloson
Stephanie Treadway Hobrock
Marissa Yip-Young
Sandy Swanger Bartles
Ruth Nixon
Sonya Steele
Melissa Adkins
Connie Heim Reynolds
Robin Coxin
Elizabeth Dent
Bonnie Littleton
Kathy Dunn
Traci Putinski
Kathleen Costa
Terri Crossley
Nickieann Fleener

Jess Dimovski
Lin Casteel-Butler
Candy Albright Kennedy
Sharleen Wells
Sharon Frank
Donna Fuller
Lynne DeBoer-Moody
Colleen Wisnom-Ladoux
Robyn Konopka
Spunky Laferrera
Melinds Lyngstad Bouwman
Verna Gass
Cindy Olmstead Russell
Tricia Dunbar
Penny Burns Marks
Barbara Tobey
Lynn Hogan
Kory Bull
Shelia Ann Wade
Doward Wilson
Joanne Kocourek
Pamela Dennis Petteway
Laura S Reading
Alice Ihnen
Donna Fuller
Kay Monk
Linda Rima
Donna Black Bates
Cindy Olmstead Russell

Books by Kathi Daley

Come for the murder, stay for the romance.

Zoe Donovan Cozy Mystery:
Halloween Hijinks
The Trouble With Turkeys
Christmas Crazy
Cupid's Curse
Big Bunny Bump-off
Beach Blanket Barbie
Maui Madness
Derby Divas
Haunted Hamlet
Turkeys, Tuxes, and Tabbies
Christmas Cozy
Alaskan Alliance
Matrimony Meltdown
Soul Surrender
Heavenly Honeymoon
Hopscotch Homicide
Ghostly Graveyard
Santa Sleuth
Shamrock Shenanigans
Kitten Kaboodle – *May 2016*

Zimmerman Academy Shorts

The New Normal
New Beginnings

Paradise Lake Cozy Mystery:

Pumpkins in Paradise
Snowmen in Paradise
Bikinis in Paradise
Christmas in Paradise
Puppies in Paradise
Halloween in Paradise

Tj Jensen Turtle Cove Mystery:

Barkley's Treasure – *April 2016*

Whales and Tails Cozy Mystery:

Romeow and Juliet
The Mad Catter
Grimm's Furry Tail
Much Ado About Felines
Legend of Tabby Hollow
Cat of Christmas Past
A Tale of Two Tabbies
The Great Catsby – *June 2016*

Seacliff High Mystery:

The Secret
The Curse
The Relic
The Conspiracy
The Grudge

Sand and Sea Hawaiian Mystery:

Murder at Dolphin Bay

Road to Christmas Romance:

Road to Christmas Past

Chapter 1

Wednesday, March 9

My name is Kailani Pope. Everyone who isn't my father or my paternal grandmother calls me Lani. Probably the most important thing you need to know about me is that I want to be a cop. Correction: I *need* to be a cop. Not only is being a proud member of the Honolulu Police Department my destiny but it's in my blood. My dad was a cop, my grandfather was a cop, my Uncle Steve is a cop, and my five brothers are all cops for various agencies within the state of Hawaii.

I know most little girls dream of being a princess, ballerina, or beauty queen when they grow up, but from the moment I was old enough to start picturing my future, I *knew* I wanted to be a cop. In the years since, I have never once wavered from my commitment to do this very thing. So why, you ask, am I *not* a cop?

You see, in spite of my unwavering determination, I have had a teeny, tiny problem making my dreams come true.

That teeny, tiny problem, as it turns out, is a teeny, tiny me. While all five of my brothers top the six-foot mark on the height charts, I have to stand on my tippy toes to even approach the five-foot mark. Although the HPD doesn't technically have a height requirement, they do have a lot more applicants than they have jobs, so it makes sense that the candidates who are most qualified, like my burly brothers, are more likely to be given the opportunity than those of us who are vertically impaired and don't quite meet the ideal prototype for police work.

I understand that a teeny, tiny cop really doesn't pose much of a threat to the oftentimes large-framed population of my home state, but I've met all the requirements set forth by the HPD and I know I could do the job better than anyone else if only the powers that be would let me try. So while I'm waiting for the growth spurt I've been praying for for the past fifteen years to finally kick in, or my name to come up on the never-ending list of qualified applicants, I work in guest services at the Dolphin Bay Resort on the north shore of Oahu as a water safety officer. Calling me a WSO is a fancy way of saying I'm a lifeguard, activities director, and babysitter all wrapped up in one.

Working for the resort isn't bad as jobs go. I get to spend the day outdoors, soaking up the sun and enjoying the tropical climate Hawaii is famous for. I work with five other WSOs, most of whom have become close and entertaining friends. The pay for a safety and rescue worker with my level of experience and training is really pretty good. When I'm not working I like to study the detective manual I lifted from my brother Jason after he finished studying for the test that moved him to the next level of the HPD food chain.

I think I'd be a good cop. What I lack in size I more than make up for in intellect and intuition. My save record as a WSO is unmatched on the island, mostly due to my ability to sense a dangerous situation before it occurs. My colleagues don't understand how I can already be in the water and on my way to the rescue before a victim even realizes they're in trouble.

"Hamilton wants you to move down to tower two."

I smiled at Cameron Carrington, my fellow lifeguard. Cam is the quintessential beach boy: tall and tan with a fit frame and blond hair that brushes his shoulders.

Probably the most outstanding things about Cam, however, are his bright blue eyes, which mirror the aqua of the sea where he spends a good deal of each and every day. Cam and I went to high school together, competed on the same swim team, joined the junior lifeguard program, and landed jobs at Dolphin Bay at about the same time. I guess you could say Cam is my best friend, along with my cousin Kekoa, who works in the hotel at the front desk.

"Okay." I got up and began gathering my belongings. "I prefer tower two anyway."

The truth of the matter is there's a lot more action on the surfing beach, where tower two is located. I feel my talents are wasted at tower one, on the family beach, but it's still a lot better than the worst assignment of all: the family pool. Whoever is assigned there needs to be long on patience, which I am not. Luckily, my boss, Mitch Hamilton, knows this and more often than not assigns me to the beach.

"Keep an eye on the riptide," Cam warned. "It's been strong all day. And there's been an unverified shark spotting from one of the surfers."

"Probably a dolphin," I countered.

"Yeah, probably, but keep an eye out anyway."

"We still on for later?" I asked as I slipped my backpack over my shoulder.

"Makena and a few of the others heard we were going to party on the beach and asked if they could join us. I told them they could. I hope that's okay."

"It's fine."

It wasn't.

I was really looking forward to having a best friend bonfire with Cam and Kekoa, but I knew he had a crush on the newest WSO team member, so if Makena wanted to hang out with us, who was I to deny him his heart's desire?

I jumped down from the tower and landed smoothly on the white sand beach. "I need to run home to grab Sandy after I get off." Sandy is a lab mix I rescued from a strong tide a few years ago. I'm not sure how he came to be in the water in the first place, but, although I looked, I was never able to find his owner. So Sandy moved in with Cam, Kekoa, and me, in the very small and very cramped condo we share. "I'll just grab the food while I'm there and meet you at the Point. I hope you told the others to bring food and beverages to contribute because I only bought enough for the three of us."

"I did. I'm not sure who all is coming. Makena said she'd fill everyone in. Maybe Brody will bring Luke."

I sent a dirty look in Cam's direction before I jogged down the beach to tower two. Brody Weller, another WSO, is an all right sort of guy except for the fact that he has a tendency to bring his very annoying best friend Luke Austin everywhere he goes. I'm not sure why Luke annoys me so much. There's just something about his huge horse ranch, perfect smile, shaggy brown hair, deep blue eyes, and southern charm that make me want to throw sand at him every time I see him. Cam thinks I have a thing for him, which I absolutely do not. There is no way I'd ever hook up with a displaced cowboy from Texas. Granted, Luke can fill out a pair of jeans better than anyone I've ever met, but the mere idea of riding a horse makes my skin itch.

No, if I was going to hook up with anyone it would be Kilohana Kapule—Kilo for short. Now there's a man after my own heart. Not only was he born and raised on the island and well away from horses but he could surf with such majesty that it seemed as if the hand of God had reached down to give him some sort of supernatural power over the forces of the sea. Of course Kilo barely knows I'm alive, but marrying the man and having his babies is definitely part of my ten-year plan, right behind becoming a cop, making detective, and winning the women's division of the Van's Triple Crown of Surfing competition.

Okay, maybe that last one is a pipe dream. I can handle myself on a board, but I'm nowhere as talented as Kilo.

"Cam told me Hamilton wants me to take over," I said to Drake Longboard, my least favorite co-worker. Not only is he much too arrogant for someone of his subpar intelligence and athletic ability but he has really long bangs that are constantly covering his eyes. He looks like a shaggy dog. The worst part of all is that he is continually, and I mean continually, running his hand through his hair to swipe it away from his face. The guy is a mess. I don't know why Hamilton hasn't made him cut his hair because I really don't know how he can see well enough to know whether anyone is drowning.

"So where am I supposed to go? I have three hours left on my shift."

I shrugged. "I have no idea. You'll have to go up to the office to ask the boss. Cam took over in tower one, so I'm guessing the family pool."

Drake grumbled the entire time he gathered his things. I ignored him as I placed my binoculars to my eyes and surveyed the situation. The family beach was protected by a reef that attracts moms and dads with their pail-toting offspring, who wade in the gentle surf and build sandcastles that will be washed away by the evening tide. In contrast, the waves on the surfing beach are pretty intense, which means it's generally occupied by surfers and the young adults who hang out watching them. Experience has shown that when you're assigned to tower two your potential victim is either going to be a tourist who really doesn't understand the power of the waves or a hot shot local who is so intent on showing off he isn't paying attention to what's going on around him.

"How long has that guy with the red trunks over by the jetty been sitting there in the sun? He's as red as a Hawaiian sunset."

"How should I know? I'm paid to watch the water, not to monitor the sunbathing habits of clueless tourists intent on baking themselves."

"You're a safety officer and it's your job to make sure our guests are both safe and happy whether they're in the water or not.

The guy looks like a lobster. Trust me, when he realizes how burned he is, he isn't going to be happy."

Drake shrugged. "What ev."

"Keep an eye on the water for one more minute while I head over to suggest he call it a day?"

Drake's only answer was in the form of a completely inappropriate comment about the man's plump belly resembling a crab rather than a lobster, but it appeared that he'd do as I asked, so I grabbed my rescue buoy and headed down the beach. I really don't know why Hamilton puts up with Drake. I mean, he's an okay WSO and he's never actually killed anyone with his lackluster attitude toward his job, but I know there are a lot of qualified people out there who would do the job better than he does, so why keep him around? Cam thinks Hamilton has a thing for Drake's aunt, Veronica, which I suppose he might. Hamilton is single and Drake's aunt is very attractive. They're about the same age and I suppose an argument could be made that the two would make a compatible couple. Still, I can't imagine being related to Drake in any way would be worth a hookup of the serious kind, even if his aunt is a babe.

"Excuse me, sir," I said as I approached the man who was laid out on a lounger with a hat over his face. "It looks like you're getting a pretty serious sunburn. It might be a good idea to call it a day."

The man didn't respond. There was an empty bar glass on the table next to the chair. It looked as if he'd been drinking our signature rum punch, which can sneak up on you if you aren't aware of the high alcohol content of the fruity drink. Chances were the guy was hammered. I can't even begin to tell you how many really serious sunburns are the result of overindulgence of alcohol combined with a day at the beach.

I used my rescue buoy to gently touch the man on the shoulder. "Sir? Can you hear me, sir? I really think it's time to head in."

The man still didn't move. I debated what to do. My instinct told me to pour water over him, but my common sense said that might make him pretty mad. After a moment's hesitation I reached over and touched the man on the shoulder. He felt cold even though it was a hot day. I was beginning to get a bad feeling about this.

I took a deep breath and prepared myself for what might happen next. "Sir," I said as I gently removed the hat from the man's face. I let out a little screech and jumped back. It was obvious from the empty stare of his open eyes that he wasn't sleeping; he was dead.

I replaced the hat over his face before instructing one of the locals to head to the tower to tell Drake to call for backup. By this point I'd attracted quite a bit of attention from lookie loos, so I focused my attention on maintaining the integrity of what I was sure was going to be declared a crime scene while I waited for someone from HPD to arrive.

"Did anyone notice if anyone was with this man?" I asked the crowd.

"He was alone when I got here and I've been here most of the day," a young woman with curly red hair answered.

It appeared the man had simply died in his sleep, most likely due to heart failure, but looks can be deceiving. My gut told me there was more going on, and my gut is rarely wrong.

"Did anyone stop by to speak to him?"

"Not that I noticed," the redhead added. "He did chat for a few minutes with the woman who brought him his drink, but that was it."

"Was the woman you're referring to one of our cocktail waitresses?"

"No; at least I don't think so. She didn't have one of the resort's uniforms on. It looked to me like she was flirting with the guy. I remember thinking she'd set her sights pretty low. She was gorgeous and this guy was...well..." She glanced at the clearly out-of-shape middle-aged man.

"Do you remember what she looked like?"

"Tall. Dark hair. Fair skinned. I didn't pay all that much attention and might not have noticed them at all if it hadn't occurred to me that the woman could do better."

I looked back toward the man whose skin was as red as his swim trunks. It amazed me that no one had tried to wake the man before I came along. If he hadn't been dead, he would have been in a whole lot of pain once the fire from the burn set in.

"What happened?" Kekoa, who must have noticed the ruckus when Hamilton was informed we had a body on the beach, came jogging over. The front desk where she works looks out onto the beach, so she's usually pretty tuned in to what's going on.

I turned my attention to my cousin. "Male victim. He was dead when I found him. I'd say he's in his late forties/early fifties. Maybe older. It's hard to tell." I lifted the edge of the hat to reveal the man's face.

Kekoa put her hand over her mouth as if to hold in vomit that was threatening to spew forth. "That's Mr. Cole. He's staying in the tower suite."

I furrowed my brow. The tower suite was our most expensive accommodation. One night in the opulent lodging costs more than an entire month's rent for the condo Kekoa and I shared with Cam. If the guy was staying there he must have been loaded. I guess that explained why a beautiful woman was trying to pick him up.

"How did he die?" Kekoa asked as she tucked long dark hair behind one ear.

"I'm not sure. It looks like he simply passed in his sleep, but my instinct tells me there's something more going on." I noticed the first HPD car pull into the parking area. I watched as my brother Jason and his partner stepped out onto the pavement. I grabbed Kekoa's hand and led her away from the crowd. Now that reinforcements had arrived I didn't feel bad about leaving my post.

"Where are we going?" Kekoa asked as she struggled to keep up with me.

I grabbed my backpack from the tower and headed toward the hotel. "I want to take a look at Cole's room before the police get to it."

"What? No. You can't. Do you know how much trouble we'll get into if someone finds out?"

"No one is going to find out. I'll be in and out as quick as a bunny."

"Are you insane? Not only will you get fired but your dad is going to kill you. And when he's done, John, Jason, Jimmy, Justin, and Jeff are *all* going to kill you too."

In case you were wondering, the *J team*, as my mom refers to them, are my brothers. I have no idea why my parents decided to give all their sons J names, especially because, although we're a traditional Hawaiian family, not one of them has a traditional Hawaiian name. I've asked on more than one occasion, and it seems the idea came from a movie. Or possibly a book. However you slice it, it's weird. And no, when I eventually persuade Kilo Kapule to first notice and then marry me, I won't be naming *any* of my children with names beginning with a J.

"I told you, they aren't going to know." I hurried across the cool tile of the lobby and slipped behind the desk. It's somewhat hard to remain inconspicuous when you're wearing a bathing suit, but everyone who was in the lobby was looking out the window, speculating about what was going on. I pushed Kekoa behind the counter and instructed her to hurry up and make a key to Cole's room.

"I'm so going to get fired," Kekoa complained as she did as I asked.

"You aren't going to get fired. I need you to watch the elevator. If you see anyone heading up to the tower suite buzz the phone in the room and I'll get out real quick."

"This isn't going to end well."

"It'll be fine."

I headed toward the elevators and pushed the button for the car that would take me directly to the top floor of the tower. I figured if I could solve this case before my brother, or anyone else, the HPD would have no choice but to take my application seriously. Jason isn't nearly as smart as I am and yet he managed to get promoted to detective. I mean really, how hard can it be?

On my way up to the suite I dug into my backpack, then slipped on a pair of shorts and the sweatshirt I'd worn that morning before it warmed up. I took out my phone, put it into my shorts pocket, and pulled the sleeves of my sweatshirt over my hands. Even Jason would think to dust for prints if it turned out foul play was involved, as I suspected it was, so I had to be sure I didn't leave any behind. I slipped my backpack back over my shoulders, then used the key Kekoa had made to enter the room.

There was an open suitcase on the bed, a laptop and several files on the desk, and a handwritten note on the bedside table next to the phone. I decided the best course of action was to photograph *everything*. I used my phone to take photos of the room in general, and then I headed over to the bed to take photos of the contents of the suitcase. When I was done there I took photos of the files on the desk. I made sure to cover my hands before touching them. I wanted to log on to the computer but it was password protected, and I really didn't have enough time to even attempt to hack my way in, so I focused my attention on the note next to the bed and the contents of the cabinet in the bathroom.

I heard my phone buzz as I turned each and every prescription pill bottle so I could take a photo of the label. I quickly e-mailed all the photos I'd taken to myself and then put my phone in my pocket. I thought I'd still have time to make my escape.

I was wrong.

I quickly slipped out of the room onto the balcony just as my brother Jason walked in. I could hear him talking to the men who were with him. They were more interested in the contents of the room than the balcony at that point, but eventually someone was going to come out to check out the exterior. I looked over the edge of the railing toward the sand, which was *very* far below. There was no way I'd survive a jump. There was another balcony directly below the one I stood on. It would be tricky to climb down without falling, and I had no way of knowing if the room was occupied or the door from the balcony open, but as I heard the men moving around inside, I realized making the climb down was really my only option.

I slowly climbed over the wrought-iron railing. I could feel my legs dangling fifteen stories above ground as I slowly walked my way down the railing with my hands. I have to say my fifty-pull-ups-a-day routine was really paying off.

When I got to the bottom of the rails I was hanging on to, I was still several feet above the balcony below. I swung my legs back and forth like I used to on the swing in the park, and then, when I knew my momentum was directed forward, I let go and sailed onto the tile floor of the balcony below.

"Wow," I said aloud. "I can't believe that actually worked."

I tried the sliding glass door that led into the room. Luckily, it was unlocked. I really didn't want to have to push my luck climbing down to the room directly below the one I'd just accessed. I slipped inside, which was, happily, deserted, and then made my way out into the hallway. I couldn't risk running into my brother or any of the other cops in the elevator, so I dragged my increasingly fatigued body toward the stairway and made the very long trip back to the lobby.

"Are you insane?" Kekoa asked after I plopped onto a stool behind the counter and recounted what had occurred. "What if you had slipped or fallen wrong when you swung yourself onto the balcony?"

"I guess I'd be dead, but I didn't slip and I'm very much alive. I need to get back to the beach before anyone realizes

I'm gone. Text me if anyone comes around asking questions about me."

I reached for my phone. It was gone. "Dang. I must have dropped my phone when I swung onto the balcony. I'm going to see if I can find it. We'll talk later."

I spent as much time as I dared looking through the shrubs at the base of the tower for my phone, but no matter how hard I tried I couldn't find it. I was beginning to regret not deleting the photos I'd taken after I e-mailed them to myself. If someone found the phone, looked at the photos, realized what they were and that the phone was mine, I'm afraid my death-defying leap of faith was going to be for nothing.

I finally gave up my search and returned to my tower, where several members of the HPD were talking to witnesses.

"So what do you think happened?" I asked Colin Reynolds, one of the officers I'd known since I was in diapers. Colin was a nice guy who had worked with my dad when he was on the force. Although I have a whole passel of real uncles, I've been referring to him as Uncle Colin for as long as I can remember.

"Too early to tell. Could be death by natural causes, but we won't know for sure until the medical examiner has a chance to check the guy out."

"What about the drink?"

"What drink?"

"The empty glass on the table. It looked like it contained rum punch at one point. I have a hunch it might have been tampered with."

Colin frowned. He held down the button on his radio and spoke into it. "Did we recover an empty glass from the table next to the victim?"

"No. There was nothing on the table next to the deceased," a voice replied back.

"But there was a glass. I saw it," I insisted.

"Joey and I arrived right behind Jason. We were one of the first teams on the scene. I don't remember seeing a glass."

I looked around the crowd. I figured the redhead I'd spoken to could vouch for the fact that Mr. Cole had had a drink delivered to him by a tall brunette but no longer saw her in the crowd. "Look, you have to trust me; there was a glass on the table. I spoke to a woman with curly red hair while I was waiting for you to show up. She said a tall brunette brought the drink to the man. She said it appeared as if the woman was flirting with him."

"A tall brunette was flirting with this man?"

"I know he doesn't look like the type to attract the attention of a beautiful woman, but he was staying in the tower suite," I informed Colin. "I'm pretty sure it runs at least several grand a night."

"Fair enough. I guess wealth trumps looks. I'll speak to the witness. Do you have a name?"

"No," I admitted.

"Do you see her here now?"

I looked around one more time. "No. She must have left. She was around five foot six with red curly hair that reached the middle of her back. She had green eyes and a southern accent. Oh, and she had on a green bikini with a wrap in a lighter shade of green. Ask around. I'm sure someone knows who she is."

"I'll do that. In the meantime, we could use your help clearing the rest of the civilians off the beach."

"Okay, I'm on it."

"And Lani…"

I turned and looked back at Colin.

"We *only* need help clearing the civilians off the beach."

"Of course. That was implied. You know I'd never meddle in your case."

I smiled the biggest and most sweetly innocent smile in my portfolio. This may be an odd thing to admit, but I've actually spent quite a bit of time in front of a mirror perfecting my facial expressions. When you have five brothers, all of whom are older and larger than you are, manipulation quickly becomes the main tool in your arsenal.

I won't say I actually meddled at this point, but I wasn't sure Colin would put much effort into trying to locate the redhead, so I asked everyone I came into contact with as I cleared the beach if they remembered seeing her. Everyone said they didn't. I also asked those nearest to where the body had been found if they remembered seeing a glass on the guy's table, but everyone I spoke to admitted they hadn't been paying much attention to the man, who'd appeared to be napping, so they hadn't really noticed.

I wasn't certain what was going on, but I had a feeling there was something going on and I intended to figure out what it was—and I meant to be the first to do so.

Chapter 2

As I mentioned, Cam, Kekoa, and I share a condo. It's really tiny and pretty run-down, but it's in a small complex, it's right on the beach, and, best of all, it's only a short bike ride away from the resort where we all work. In other words, in spite of the fact that Kekoa and I have to share a bedroom and Cam is a complete and total slob, it's perfect.

When I got home after my shift I changed into a yellow bikini and a pair of faded cutoffs. Then I slipped my feet into bright yellow flip-flops, shoved a clean sweatshirt into my backpack, pulled my long dark hair into a sloppy ponytail, and began loading my car with my surfboard and the food and drink I'd bought for our cookout.

The Shell Beach Condominiums, where we live, has six units, numbered one through six. Cam, Kekoa, and I live in unit 1, which is the first condo along the sidewalk that leads to the parking area. Kekoa wanted to wait for a unit to open up that would have less foot traffic, but I like being in a positon to watch my neighbors as they come and go. I guess you could say I'm nosy.

Everyone in the other five units is very nice and we all get along fabulously, except for Mr. B in unit 6. Mr. B never seems to leave his condo and never talks to anyone. In fact, I personally have never met the man. He hasn't lived in the building long—maybe a month—but it's my opinion, based on his behavior, that he's hiding out from someone, and as far as I'm concerned, that makes him interesting. Cam thinks he's just an introvert and doesn't enjoy social interactions, but I think there's something more going on. I haven't yet determined if he's a good guy hiding out from the bad guys or a bad guy hiding out from the cops, but I've been working on a plan first to introduce myself and then slowly integrate myself into his life so I can find out what's really going on once and for all.

As you may be able to discern, I have an active curiosity that at times lands me in a heap of trouble. Which could be another reason the HPD hasn't moved me to the top of the waiting list for a spot on the team. I've never intentionally broken any laws, but there have been moments when my inclination to snoop has come to the attention of my brothers and their cop colleagues, and in all fairness, I supposed I could see how these incidents could hurt my chances of being offered the job my heart longs for.

It's not that I wake up in the morning and ask myself what sort of trouble I can get into. It's more that I'm impulsive and tend to act first and think later. There are times when this tendency toward spontaneity has worked well for me and lives have been saved, and there have been others when my well-intended actions have landed me in a heap of trouble.

I made sure that the door to the condo was firmly closed, then called to my yellow lab, Sandy, who was chasing seagulls on the beach. I buckled Sandy into the passenger seat of my Jeep and headed toward one of the best surfing spots in the area. The most awesome thing about this particular beach is that it's off the beaten path, and most tourists don't even know it exists.

When I arrived I was happy to see the waves were just about perfect. It was sunny and warm but not too hot, as it can be at times. The swells started in the distance and then rolled in toward the beach in perfectly synchronized sets that would make planning for the perfect wave all that much easier.

There's nothing better than riding a giant wave in the warm tropical water as the sun sets behind you. I've participated in many different activities in my life, but I haven't found a single thing that can take you away from your problems and help calm your mind more completely than racing across the sea as the wave curls and crashes into the water just behind you. Well, maybe sex, but it would be impolite to bring that up here.

I unbuckled Sandy and instructed him to hop down from the Jeep. I grabbed my board and backpack and headed over to the fire that someone had already built.

"Did you bring the beer?" Cam asked.

"Ice chest in the back of my Jeep. I'm surprised you aren't in the water. It's about as perfect as it can get."

"I'm going to head in, but I thought I'd wait for Makena. She should be here any time."

I shrugged and tossed my backpack on the sand next to where Cam was sitting. "Your loss. You may as well unload both ice chests while you're waiting."

I tucked my board under my arm and ran toward the water with Sandy chasing along behind me. Given the fact that I work on the beach and spend a significant amount of my free time surfing, I spend a *lot* of time in the ocean. There are times I worry about what all that saltwater will do to my hair and skin, but when it comes right down to it, the ocean is where I feel most at home.

I noticed Brody had shown up with Luke. I did my best to ignore them, not because the very sight of Luke makes my teeth hurt from all the clenching I do to keep my less-than-flattering opinions about him to myself but because Brody is a wave hog. The guy is only a moderately skilled surfer, yet he seems to think any wave is fair game whether someone else already has claimed it or not. I'm pretty good at avoiding what might appear to be an inevitable collision, but one of these days Brody is going to hurt someone with his wave hog ways and I'd really prefer that *someone* not be me.

By the time I decided to call it a day and return to the fire, the rest of the gang had arrived. Cam was sitting on a blanket next to Makena, trying not to be obvious about the fact that he was staring at her breasts, Drake was shooting the breeze with Brody and Luke, who both looked bored by whatever story he was telling, and Kekoa was talking to Tessa, the smartest of all the WSOs next to me. I've seen Brody noticing Tessa when he thinks no one is looking, but I'd be willing to bet my favorite surfboard that he has little to no chance with the serious and ambitious woman who is simply biding her time until she earns enough money to head to the mainland and pursue the college degree she's always yammering on about. Personally, I don't know why anyone would want to spend four years of their life in a stuffy classroom, but Tessa seems as committed to her dream of going to college as I do to mine of becoming a cop.

"Figures that the most excitement that's happened at the resort in a good long while happens when I'm off," Brody complained as I grabbed my towel and dried myself off.

"It's rude to refer to the death of one of our guests as excitement," Kekoa pointed out. "Mr. Cole deserves our respect."

"Cole?" Luke asked. "Are you referring to Branson Cole?"

"Yeah," Kekoa answered. "Do you know him?"

Luke nodded. "He's quite good friends with my father. How did he die?"

"It's inconclusive at this point, but I'm going to go out on a limb and say he was drugged," I answered as I pulled my sweatshirt over my head. "Or at least that's my theory based on the fact that he had an empty glass beside him that seems to have disappeared before HPD was able to retrieve it. I mean, why take the glass unless it was to hide evidence?"

"I thought he died in his sleep," Drake countered.

"That's what everyone was saying at the scene, but the guy's eyes were wide open when I lifted the hat off his face and his features were somewhat distorted. I'm betting he died in some degree of pain but was unable to move or even call out for help. If you ask me, whatever drug was added to his drink paralyzed him before it killed him."

"Ew. Do you need to be so graphic?" Makena complained.

I rolled my eyes. I really didn't know what Cam saw in the newest member of our little group. She's such a girl.

"If he was drugged, do you happen to know if the HPD has made an arrest?" Luke continued.

"Not as far as I've heard." I made myself a plate of the food that had been set out on the table. The selection of fresh fish that had been grilled to perfection indicated that Brody had used his time off to do a little spearfishing.

"Based on the deep furrow in Jason's forehead when I saw him just prior to leaving the resort for the day, I'd say the ME confirmed my suspicion about drugs contributing to the man's death. I also think he's confused by my report about there being a glass on the table next to where the guy was sitting, and he's been unsuccessful in tracking down the redheaded witness and the woman who brought over the drink." I looked directly at Luke. "You know the guy; do you have any idea who might want him dead?"

Luke didn't answer right away, but I could tell he was seriously considering my question. I supposed I shouldn't be surprised that Luke knew Branson Cole. Cole was rich and Luke came from a wealthy family. It had always seemed to me that the rich and influential among us tended to form a pretty tight bond that seemed to exist for the express purpose of keeping the less affluent at arm's length.

"Do you know how long Branson had been on the island?" Luke asked.

"He checked into the tower suite three days ago," Kekoa supplied. "I'm not sure if he had just arrived on the island or if he stayed somewhere else before his reservation with us."

Luke pulled his phone out of his backpack and headed down to the water's edge. I watched as he paced back and forth, talking to someone. The sun had set some time ago so it was dark, but the moon provided just enough light for me to see Luke running his hand through his hair in a fairly agitated manner. Luke had said he knew the man. Maybe he *did* know who'd killed him.

Luke himself had arrived on the scene almost two years earlier. I'm not sure how he got hooked up with Brody, who's a very different kind of person than Luke appears to be. Not that I really knew Luke all that well. Sure, he seemed to pop up at a lot of the same events I attended, but I went out of my way to avoid him, so I'd really only said a handful of words to him in all the time I'd known him. I'd noticed Luke watching me from time to time with a serious look of contemplation on his face. I'm not sure what was going on in that head of his, but I found the whole thing to be both creepy and oddly exciting.

"Looks like Kilo made it after all," Cam announced just as I was on the verge of ripping my brain out for admitting even to myself that I found Luke somewhat exciting.

My heart filled with anticipation as I turned toward the parking lot in anticipation of the arrival of the love of my life. Kilo was absolutely perfect for me and I was sure we'd enjoy many years of happiness together. Now I just needed to get him to notice me. My whole being was immersed with happiness as he stepped out of his car. God, he was a babe. But that happiness turned to anger when I saw him walking around the car to open the passenger door. He held out a hand to a bleached blond bimbo who caused quite the disturbance among the guys in the crowd as her fit but voluptuous body came into view.

What is it with busty blondes and men anyway? Working at the resort, I've witnessed men of all ages make fools of themselves as they panted after some silicone-enhanced Barbie doll while their wives looked on in anger. They're on vacation in one of the most romantic places in the world with the women they'd pledged to spend their lives with. Shouldn't their focus be on them and only them?

I was never settling down unless I could pull off a miracle and convince Kilo to marry me and forsake all others. I knew a lot of men, but in my humble opinion there wasn't one that would be worth all the trouble that seemed to come with tying the knot. Don't get me wrong; I like to date, and I do so fairly often, but marriage? Thanks but no thanks.

Right about the time Kilo announced he was taking Barbie—not her real name—to Australia with him for an upcoming surf competition, I decided I really needed a walk. I thought about telling someone where I was going, but all eyes and ears were on Kilo, so I motioned for Sandy to follow me and started down the beach.

I knew I should give up on Kilo. He barely knew I was alive and he certainly didn't see me in the way I wanted him to. But I kept thinking he'd tire of dating supermodels and turn his sights elsewhere. I'd tried to be patient and wait for him to realize the best life partner is one with whom you share a background and common interests. I'd bet Barbie didn't know how to surf, spear a fish, or free dive for shellfish. What could the man possibly see in her?

I stopped and stared at the water. The tide had turned and the waves had gentled quite a bit. The moon had risen higher in the sky and was shining down on the water, providing a nice glow in the otherwise dark night. Maybe I should just go home. I had my own car and my enthusiasm for the evening had waned considerably after Kilo arrived with his date.

"Beautiful night." Luke walked up and stood beside me.

"It's all right." I shrugged. "Was that your dad you were talking to?"

"Yeah. He was pretty upset to hear about Branson but not all that surprised."

Okay. Now that had my attention. "Why wasn't he surprised?"

"He mentioned that Branson had gotten wrapped up in a business deal that appeared to be less than legit. Bran wanted my dad to invest in his project, but after doing his due diligence my dad decided to pass."

"What kind of business?"

"He's part of an investment group that's planning to build a resort not far from Dolphin Bay. My dad commented that on the surface the project looked to be potentially profitable, but it's his opinion that the seed money is dirty, and he wanted no part in it. He also mentioned that there were some zoning issues that as far as he knew had never been resolved, as well as backlash from local environmental groups. In his opinion the whole thing wasn't likely ever to get off the ground, and even if it did, he didn't need the hassle."

"Does your dad know the identity of the people involved in the project?"

"Branson never said who he was in business with, but I got the feeling my dad has an idea who might be involved. He also told me Branson said he was spending time with a woman who lived on the island. Apparently she's significantly younger than Bran and quite the looker, so he'd been bragging about his new relationship to anyone who would listen. Her first name is Helena, but that's all my dad knew."

I sat down on a nearby rock as I tried to figure out my next move. I really wanted to solve this case before the HPD. I felt I had been handed a chance to show them what I could do and I didn't want to waste it, even if that meant I would have to work with Luke.

I turned toward him and looked directly into his eyes. "I've decided to look into Mr. Cole's murder myself. I could use some help if you're interested."

I hated Luke just a tiny bit less when he didn't laugh or even question the fact that I intended to investigate.

"Are you working tomorrow?"

"No, I'm off," I answered.

"Then why don't you come out to the ranch? I'll make you lunch and we can talk."

"The ranch? The place you keep the horses?"

Luke laughed. "Don't tell me the fearless Lani Pope is afraid of horses."

"I'm not afraid of anything. I seem to have misplaced my phone, so I need to replace it first thing in the morning, but I can be out to your place by eleven."

"Eleven works fine. Bring Sandy. I think he'll get along well with my dogs. Maybe we can take a walk along the bluff, or even ride—if you're brave enough."

I wanted to say I was brave enough to do anything, but I wasn't sure *anything* included climbing up on top of a smelly beast that had the power to toss me off its back and stomp me to death. I really don't get the fascination so many people have with these four-legged modes of transportation. It never ceases to amaze me that the number-one extra our guests want to add to their resort package next to a luau is horseback riding on the beach. Really? Horseback riding? You would think our guests would be more interested in learning to surf or scuba dive, but the horses win out every time.

I stood up and wiped the sand from the back of my shorts before turning my attention back to Luke. "When's the last time you spoke to Mr. Cole?"

Luke furrowed his brow, and I hated to admit it, but he really was good-looking doing it. His smile was wide and inviting, the dimple on the right side of his mouth seemed to draw your attention every time he spoke, and his blue eyes were framed with thick dark lashes that had half the women on the island panting after him. Like I said before, and I will say again, I have absolutely no use for any man who is, in my opinion, just a bit too perfect. Still, on more than one occasion, I'd found myself picturing him shirtless, wearing nothing but low-riding jeans and cowboys boots like the models they use in aftershave ads.

"It's been quite a while actually," Luke finally said. "He came around on a regular basis when I was a kid, but then I went off to college and didn't get home much."

"And after college?"

"I moved to New York."

I know I made a face that clearly communicated my disdain for his choice of residence. "Why in the world would a country boy from Texas move to New York?"

"This country boy got a job as a stockbroker. My time in the Big Apple provided a lifestyle that was completely different from anything I'd ever known, but I loved it. There's something about that city. It has its own energy and I got caught up in the vitality of the place. I worked hard, I partied hard, I took huge risks with my money, and I made a killing. Don't get me wrong: I know the risks I took could have gone either way, and I wouldn't recommend the particular portfolio I developed for myself to anyone else, but it worked for me. I made enough money in less than a decade to live comfortably for the rest of my life."

I dug my toes into the sand as the wave that had just rolled onto the sand covered my feet. I'd assumed Luke's daddy had bought him the horse ranch. I guess it made me feel moderately better about him if he'd actually worked hard and earned the money himself. But just barely. The man still spent the bulk of his time around horses, and that I would never understand.

I picked up a shell and tossed it into the receding water. "So how did you end up living on a horse ranch on Oahu?"

"I woke up one day and realized my lifestyle was killing me. Literally. I was only thirty years old and I'd developed high blood pressure and insomnia. I decided to cash out and return to a simpler way of living before it was too late."

"Okay, so why Hawaii?"

Luke stopped walking. He turned and looked out toward the sea. "Texas was a great place to grow up, but when I asked myself where out of all the places I'd spent time in my life I'd most like to live, I realized it was here. Hawaii is the antithesis of New York. While Manhattan generates a feverish energy you can almost hear and most definitely feel, Hawaii is slow and calming. The lifestyle that can be had on the islands seems almost devoid of urgency. I could feel my blood pressure drop the moment I stepped off the plane."

I totally got what Luke was saying. There *was* something really calming about living your life on island time. As for me, I couldn't imagine it any other way.

I could hear the others laughing in the distance. I was never going to live down the sly remarks and innuendos if I spent much more time alone with the man I'd made clear to everyone was my archnemesis and mortal enemy. I quickly said my good-byes, grabbed my stuff before anyone took the time to notice who I had been with, and headed toward my Jeep.

I willed my racing heart to slow as I made the drive home. I really felt nothing but disdain for Luke, and yet our conversation had served to make him just a bit more tolerable in my eyes. Still, there was no way I was going to let Cam be right about me having a thing for him. I'd let him help me solve this case and then I'd go back to avoiding and ignoring him.

I decided a long time ago that if I decided to marry—and that was a big if—I was going to marry a Hawaiian boy from a good family who would understand the history and traditions I'd been brought up with and were still very important to me. Sure, I'd dated my share of white guys who thought hula was nothing more than a dance or a roasted pig nothing more than a meal, but those meaningless flirtations were nothing more than that: meaningless.

As I unloaded the Jeep I noticed something odd. It appeared as if unit 6 was dark. It was never dark. Mr. B had heavy drapes that he kept closed 24-7, but at night you could hear the sound of his television through the open window and see the outline of the light from his living room around the edges of the curtains. Tonight there was nothing.

After I set my belongings in the condo and tiptoed along the walkway to the opposite end I stood outside the window and listened. I didn't hear the sound of a television or a person moving around or anything else. I was tempted to knock on the door, but I didn't have a good reason for doing so, and he might simply have retired early. Each condo came with a single garage space and the door to his was closed, so there was no way to tell if his vehicle was on the premises or not. I went back to my condo and stood on the lanai in front of it, staring down the row toward unit 6. There must be some way to find out if Mr. B had left the building for the first time since he'd been living there or if he'd simply decided to turn in early.

My next-door neighbor, Elva Talbot, was home. Elva didn't drive and rarely went out at night unless she was with a friend. I could hear the sound from her television, so I assumed this wasn't one of those nights. She, like me, enjoyed keeping tabs on the comings and goings of the other residents of the complex, so I knocked on her door and asked if it was okay to come in.

"Lani, how are you, dear? I hoped you'd stop by."

"You did?" I sat down on the sofa across from the woman who more than filled out the large lounger on which she sat. Elva was a senior woman who had lived in the condominium building longer than any of the current residents. Although she wasn't one to talk about her past, I knew that at one time she'd had both a husband and a daughter. It seemed, based on the tidbits I'd managed to gather and piece together, her daughter Emily was killed in an automobile accident when she was just eight and her husband, who had been driving at the time of the accident, never had recovered from the guilt and grief. After quite a few years of trying to make a marriage out of the debris that had been left by their daughter's passing, the couple had divorced and Elva's husband had moved off the island.

"I heard you found a dead man on the beach today." Elva's face, red with excitement, seemed to clash with the orange and yellow of the muumuu she wore. "I want to hear all about it. Don't leave out a single detail. It's not often we have so much excitement on our end of the island."

I spent the next twenty minutes filling Elva in on the details of what had occurred without saying anything that might incriminate me regarding my activities immediately after my discovery of Branson Cole's body. Elva encouraged me to take my time and be specific in the telling of the tale. I suppose I could see how the recanting of the details of a murder scene could be the highlight of the woman's week. Other than Mondays, when I drove her into town for lunch with her friends, followed by senior bingo, the woman rarely went anywhere.

When I felt I had exhausted the subject I asked about Mr. B, who Elva confirmed had left his apartment earlier that afternoon. I had to wonder if Branson Cole's death and Mr. B's decision to leave his apartment for the first time we knew of were in any way related. Elva hadn't spoken to Mr. B and really had no idea where he had gone or when he might return.

"It's been quite the day, I'll say that," Elva concluded. "Did you hear there's a new tenant in unit three?"

"No, I hadn't. Who moved in?"

"A lovely young woman named Mary and her adopted Hawaiian daughter, Malia. I'd say Malia is around ten or so."

"The apartment was dark when I walked by."

"They were here today to look at the condo. Mary mentioned they'd be moving in over the weekend. It'll be nice to have a young one around. I do so miss the sound of children playing on the beach."

"Yeah." I placed my hand over Elva's and gave it a squeeze. "I can't wait to meet them."

I spoke to her for a few more minutes and then returned to my condo. I felt sorry for the lonely woman who had been through so much sadness in her life. Elva was the sort to always present a joyful exterior, but I'd been around her long enough to recognize the grief that often clouded her eyes.

I logged onto my laptop to confirm that the photos I'd e-mailed myself had come through clearly. Luckily, they had. Now that I'd lost my phone they were the only copies I had.

I slowly worked my way through the photos in an attempt to see if anything obvious jumped out at me. There didn't seem to be anything all that interesting in the suitcase on Mr. Cole's bed. The note on the table next to the phone simply had a date—tomorrow's date, to be specific— the number 4, which I assumed meant four o'clock, and the name of a locals' bar that was quite a way inland and off the beaten path. I supposed the four could refer to something else altogether, but I didn't think I was going out on a limb in thinking Branson Cole was meeting someone at the Jungle Bar at four in the afternoon the following day. It couldn't hurt, I supposed, to stop by for a drink and a look around.

I studied the photos of the items I'd found in the bathroom. It looked like Cole was on a lot of medication. I'm not an expert on prescription drugs, so I had no idea if anything he was taking could relate to his death. I made a list and vowed to find out.

I supposed before I got too far ahead of myself I should confirm that Branson Cole's death actually could have been caused by some sort of chemical added to his drink. The missing glass indicated to me that something was going on; still, I didn't want to waste a bunch of time chasing windmills. Chances were Jason had a copy of the ME report on his home computer. It was his habit to keep copies of important documents relating to open cases at home so he could check things out if something occurred to him while he was off duty. It just so happened that I knew the password to his home computer, so all I needed to do was pop in to say hi and then come up with a way to access the computer while no one was looking.

Chapter 3

Thursday, March 10

I decided to get an early start the next morning. I had a lot I wanted to accomplish before I headed out to the ranch to meet Luke at eleven. I greeted the day as I do most days with a run along the beach with Sandy, followed by a series of sun salutations as the sun rises into the sky. One of the things I love most about my island home is the connection to nature I experience each time I ride a giant wave, watch the sun rise or set, or hike along an isolated trail in the tropical paradise that few others have traveled. There's a natural rhythm that permeates the culture that really isn't duplicated anywhere else in the world. I guess I don't really know that for a fact because I've never really been anywhere, but I've overheard tourists make that comment time and time again.

I finished my yoga routine and returned to the condo, put on a pot of coffee, and headed to the ˉshower. Both Cam and Kekoa had shifts at the resort but neither had to check in until ten and neither tended to be an early riser. I normally enjoy the early mornings, when I have the condo and beach to myself. It's easy to get so caught up in the everyday moments of your life that you forget to pause and enjoy the peace and beauty around you. I once took a class with a yoga instructor who encouraged us to stand in meditation and then turn to face each of the four directions: north, east, south, and west. As we faced each, we were to verbally thank the universe for something we'd experienced that made us happy or in some way brought joy to our lives. I can't say I do that every day, but it wouldn't be at all unusual to hear me thank Mother Nature for the scent of the flowers that grow near our condo, the sound of the waves as they break on the beach, the sight of the whales in the distance, or the feel of the white sand under my feet.

I dressed in casual shorts, a tank top, and comfortable tennis shoes, poured a cup of coffee, and headed out onto the lanai in front of the condo. It looked like it was going to be another perfect day in paradise and I for one couldn't wait to get started. The phone store didn't open until ten and I was supposed to meet Luke at eleven, so if I wanted to stop by Jason's I was going to have to do it first. Chances were Jason had gone into work early because he had a murder case to solve, and my sister-in-law, Alana, usually took my niece and nephew to school at around nine, so it made sense that the best time to pay a visit to my brother's home was just as Alana was leaving. She'd tell me she had to run the kids to school, I'd offer to wait, I'd hack into Jason's computer during the fifteen minutes or so it took Alana to take the kids to school, share a quick cup of coffee with the woman I really did adore when she returned, and then make my excuses and head to the phone store.

The plan seemed solid and in theory shouldn't have posed any problems except that when I arrived at Jason's house Alana had already left. Luckily, the back door leading out onto the patio was rarely locked during the day, so I hopped the fence and let myself in. Then I unlocked the front door and let Sandy in. If it came up, I would simply claim the front door was open when I arrived so I decided to wait.

I left Sandy in the kitchen with Jason's dog Kali and headed down the tiled hallway to my brother's office. It only took me a few minutes to log onto his computer. Sure enough, there was a file on his desktop labeled *Cole*. I opened it and went straight to the medical examiner's report. If Alana had left early to take the kids to school, she might be home early as well. I thought about e-mailing the file to myself, but I was afraid Jason might notice that, so I grabbed a pen and a piece of paper and jotted down a few notes.

It appeared as if the ME had found, among other things, Tetrodotoxin, histamine, tryptamine, octopamine, taurine, acetylcholine, and accelerated levels of dopamine in Cole's system. Most everything that was found could be explained by natural occurrences in the body combined with the prescription drugs he took with the exception of the Tetrodotoxin. According to the ME, Tetrodotoxin was a neurotoxin associated with pufferfish, ocean sunfish, triggerfish, and blue-ringed octopus among other inhabitants of the ocean. According to the report, the toxin could enter the body of a victim by ingestion, injection, inhalation, or through abraded skin.

I couldn't help but think about the missing glass. Was it possible the venom had been added to the drink? I needed to do some more research to know for certain, so I made a note of the chemicals and slipped it into my pocket. Then I logged off the computer and slipped into the sunny kitchen just as Alana arrived home.

"What are you doing here?" Alana hugged me in welcome.

"I wanted to borrow that yellow top you bought the last time we went shopping for my date this evening," I improvised. "When I realized I missed you I decided to wait."

"I'm glad you did. It's been forever since we had a chance to catch up. Who's the date with?"

"Just a tourist I met at the resort. It's nothing serious, but I figured if the guy wanted to buy me an expensive dinner I'd let him."

Alana set her purse on the counter. "You should really be careful dating guys you don't know. There are a lot of weirdos out there."

I shrugged. "I know, but this guy seems harmless and I can take care of myself. So can I borrow the top?"

"Sure. I'll get it. Help yourself to some coffee."

I decided I had time for a quick cup. Alana would think it odd if I didn't stay to chat for a few minutes at least. I didn't really have a date that evening, but I could always use a hair appointment or something girlie as an excuse to make my escape if our chat went too long. Besides, maybe she knew something about Jason's investigation. It couldn't hurt to casually ask.

Jason and Alana lived in a nice house in a nice neighborhood. The house was large enough so that each of their two children had their own bedroom and there was additional space for Jason's office and Alana's sewing room. The house wasn't on the beach, which would be a deal killer for me, but they did have a large lot with a pool and a BBQ area where they entertained quite often. Honestly, living in a middle-class neighborhood where every house is similar to the next wouldn't be my thing at all, but as far as I could tell the family seemed happy with their living arrangements.

Alana came back downstairs with the top in her hand.

"Thanks so much. I'm sure I could have dug up something in my closet, but from the moment I was invited to dinner all I could think about was how awesome this top would look with that new floral skirt I bought."

"The top will look good with the skirt and I'm happy to lend it to you. I could, however, use a favor in return."

"Sure. Anything."

"Do you remember Jennifer Branton?"

"Your college roommate? Yeah. What about her?"

"She's vacationing on the island and has invited Jason and me to dinner a week from Saturday. I don't suppose you could babysit?"

"I'd be happy to as long as it's after my shift. I don't get off until seven."

"Seven will work. I'll make a reservation for eight. Hopefully Jason will have his murder investigation wrapped up by then. If history is any indication, I won't be seeing much of him until he closes the case. He left for work at six this morning with instructions not to wait up."

"He does tend to get pretty intense when he's working on a case. Does it seem like he has any leads?"

"I don't know. He didn't say, but he didn't seem happy, so I'm thinking no. Hopefully something will break today. He said he had a few ideas he wanted to check in to, so maybe they'll pan out."

"For your sake I hope so." I crossed the tile floor with my mug of coffee, then sat down at the small table nestled in the kitchen nook. Alana followed me.

"Jason said you were the one to discover the man was dead."

"Yeah." I added a dollop of milk to the dark brew. "He was on Drake's beach and he didn't even notice the guy was burned to a crisp. Maybe if he had checked it out sooner he could have helped him."

"Drake is pretty self-involved, but there probably wasn't anything he could have done. Based on what Jason said, the man didn't even try to get up, so it must have been quick."

"Yeah, I guess. Still, it seems odd that someone could die in the middle of a crowd and not a single person noticed anything."

"Crowds can create a sense of isolation. There are so many people around that no one feels responsible for anyone else. There's a tendency to build an invisible wall around yourself and the people you're with. It's sad that the man couldn't get help before it was too late, but I suppose not really all that surprising."

I hated to think Alana was right, but what she said did seem to make sense. It was the same in the water. There could be a hundred people swimming and body boarding when one person got into trouble, yet there were so many times no one responded or even seemed to notice until the lifeguard or WSO dashed into the water to make the rescue.

"Are you guys going to be at Mom's for the barbecue on Sunday?" I asked.

"The kids and I are planning on it. Jason's presence will depend on whether he feels he needs to work or not."

"The brothers are all coming, so I know Mom will be disappointed if Jason doesn't make it. You should really try to talk him into it even if this case isn't wrapped up."

"Is Jeff bringing Candy?"

"He is as far as I know. I have to say, I wasn't really into the party when Mom first mentioned it, but now that I know Candy will be there I wouldn't miss it for the world."

"I wasn't aware you were such a big fan of Candy."

"I'm not. But I am a big fan of the fireworks that will erupt when Jeff shows up with her."

Jeff is my youngest brother and Candy is the good-for-nothing, two-timing whore who broke his heart. At least according to my mother. The truth of the matter is that Jeff and Candy began dating in high school and the decision to spilt after graduation was mutual. They really did seem to care for each other, but they realized they were too young to be in such a serious relationship and felt it best to part ways. The main problem was that Candy moved on right away while Jeff mourned the loss of something he held dear, so in my mom's mind Candy was the reason they didn't get back together after they had a chance to think things through. Who knows, maybe Mom was right; it did seem Jeff regretted the decision they'd made once he took a step back and realized what it was he'd given up.

"I'm sure Jason will try to come if he can. I know he enjoys these family gatherings, but I also know he has big goals and really puts a lot into his job," Alana commented.

"Yeah. He really does."

Suddenly I felt bad for wanting to solve the case before him. It wasn't that I wanted to show him up exactly; it was more that I wanted to be given credit for my knowledge and skills.

"Listen, I have some errands to do, so I need to head out. Thanks for the use of the top and I'll be sure to put that Saturday on my schedule. Seems like it's been a while since I spent any time with Kala and Kale."

"The kids will be excited as well. I'm pretty sure next to Jason and me, Aunt Lani is their favorite person."

I smiled. Kala and Kale, six-year-old twins, are two of my very favorite people too. Being the youngest of six children, I was always the baby, and being the only girl of the six, I was spoiled and pampered from day one. I never really had a desire for a younger sibling, and when I got to be old enough to earn some extra money babysitting, I tended to pass. In fact, until the birth of Kala and Kale, I was pretty sure children weren't in my future, but after spending time with the adorable twins I've begun to open my mind to the possibility. In the very distant future of course.

My mom seems fine with the fact that my brothers, with the exception of Jason, are all single, but she's been hounding me to find a guy, settle down, and provide some grandbabies almost since I finished high school. I don't really get the double standard. Kekoa thinks my mom wants me to find someone who will take care of me, but I'm going to state outright that Kailani Pope can take care of herself.

The trip from Jason's back into town was pretty quick. Luckily, the phone store wasn't crowded, and once I wrote them a ridiculously large check, they replaced my phone with not only a new one but a newer model. By the time I finally completed all the paperwork required for the upgrade, it was time to head toward Luke's ranch. I wasn't going to have time to go home to change, so I hoped shorts and casual tennis shoes wouldn't be frowned upon on the upper-class part of the island.

The drive along the coast toward Luke's ranch was along one of the most beautiful parts of the island. The land Luke had purchased was on a bluff overlooking the water and I assumed he'd paid a mint for it. After our talk the previous evening I had to wonder how much money Luke actually had made from his high-risk portfolio. He didn't seem to have a current source of income, so I imagined his investments must still be paying off quite nicely.

I turned off the main road and onto the private one leading to the house. White fences surrounded bright green fields where horses grazed on the tall grass. Luke didn't have a lot of horses, maybe ten, and he didn't seem to do anything with the ones he had. I'd never heard him mention racing or breeding, so I thought he must keep them for their entertainment value.

The house was a low-lying ranch style that seemed to sprawl in all directions. I'd been to Luke's place once before with Brody, so I knew there was a large pool and patio area behind the house. The barn was set away from the house but was accessible via a paved footpath. I supposed it might be nice to live in a house where the bathroom alone was larger than my condo, but Sandy and I really didn't need anything more than we had.

I parked my old Jeep in the drive behind Luke's new truck. I unbuckled Sandy and we headed up the walk to the front door. I rang the bell and only had to wait a moment for Luke to answer. Standing behind him were two golden retrievers he introduced as Duke and Dallas.

Once we were comfortable the dogs were going to get along, Luke led me to the patio, where he'd set up a table near the pool for our lunch. The pool had a large waterfall spilling into it on one end that reminded me of the natural falls Kekoa and I had hiked to on Kauai the previous summer. I could see Luke had gone to a lot of trouble to incorporate native plants around the pool that really gave you the feeling of being smack dab in the middle of a tropical jungle. The patio itself was made of a dark brown tile that contrasted with the white sand surrounding it in a very aesthetic manner.

Ono sandwiches and a fresh fruit salad that looked as if they'd been prepared in the kitchen of a fine restaurant were waiting on a waterside table. Maybe they had. "This looks delicious," I said. Luke certainly seemed to be able to afford a personal chef and I'd seen his kitchen when Brody had brought me by; it was magnificent.

I sat down at the table, which had been placed in the shade of a large palm and looked out toward the ocean in the distance. The view wasn't as awesome as being right on the beach like my condo was, but it was pretty darn nice. When you added in the green from the pastures and the lush foliage it was a beautiful spot to have a meal.

"So how many horses do you have?" I asked after I served myself.

"Twelve. Actually thirteen as of two days ago, when Lucifer was born."

"Lucifer?"

"The newest addition to my stable. Would you like to meet him after lunch?"

Surprisingly, I realized I would. I really, really hated horses, but how terrifying could a two-day-old foal be?

Luke and I chatted about the remodel he'd been doing to the house, his future plans for his stable, and general conversation about the island and the people we knew while we ate. I found him to be a lot more interesting than I ever imagined he would or could be. I mean, his best friend was Brody, who was a nice guy but a total slacker and a bit of a screwup. I guess I just figured if Luke was as rich as he appeared to be and still wanted to hang out with Brody, he must be nothing more than a spoiled kid who avoided responsibility and lived off his dad's money. The past twenty-four hours had been a real eye-opener.

"How did you and Brody become friends? On the surface the two of you don't seem to have much in common."

"Brody and I met when we collided on a wave."

I laughed. Brody *was* a wave hog.

"My first instinct was to deck the guy not only for stealing my wave but for almost killing me in the process. But he seemed so genuinely sincere in his apology that I decided to let it go. He invited me for a beer, I accepted, and we got to talking. We had a really good time. I'd just moved to the island and didn't know anyone, while Brody had grown up here and knew everyone. He offered to introduce me around, and when I found out he was living in his car, I offered to let him stay in my pool house until he got on his feet. That was two years ago."

"Let me guess: he still lives in the pool house."

Luke smiled. "Yeah, he does. I know he's probably taking advantage of our friendship, but he's a good guy and we have fun together. We each have our own space, yet if I want to share a beer at the end of the day there's someone to join me. It's worked out for both of us."

"You know that unless you kick him out he's going to live here until they take him away in a body bag?"

"Yeah, I know, but it's working for now, and if at some point it stops working, I guess I'll deal with it. How's the ono."

"It's fabulous. Did you grill it yourself?"

"Of course. If there's one thing a Texan knows how to do it's grill anything and everything."

I hated to admit it, but I was having the best time in spite of the horses running freely just across the pasture. Of course I wasn't here to be pampered, I was here to work. "Were you able to dig up any new information on the project Cole was working on?"

"Actually I was. It turns out the resort project is being proposed by a development firm known as CAD Development."

"Cad?"

"Cole, Anderson, and Devlin. I looked into the financial position of all three men and it's obvious they were being backed by investors not listed on the incorporation papers. At this point I have no idea who they might be or what they might have at risk if the development falls through."

"It might fall through?"

"It just might. CAD Development purchased the land they plan to build the resort on but haven't yet obtained all the permits they'll need to continue with the project. Or at least they hadn't obtained them as of the report I found, which was dated ten days ago. In all fairness, I suppose things could have changed, but I sort of doubt it. The main stumbling block, as far as I can tell, is from groups that have petitioned the court to put a stop to the development based on a number of environmental issues."

"So, theoretically, Cole and associates could very well have spent the money the investors put up and not be able to follow through with the project."

"Theoretically."

"I guess they could sell the land and cut their losses if the construction is blocked."

"They could," Luke agreed, "but if the environmental groups are successful in blocking construction the land will be worth a fraction of what CAD paid for it."

I supposed that made sense. The reason it was such a highly valued piece of land was due to the fact that it would make a killer location for a high-end resort. Once the project was shut down it would be pretty much impossible to remarket the property as land that could be developed for this purpose. "Okay, so who are we suspecting in Cole's murder? If it was one of the environmentalists who was killed I would suspect Cole, Anderson, Devlin, or one of the investors, but who stands to benefit from Cole's death?"

"I'm not sure yet. I haven't had a lot of time to dig around, but it's a start. How about you? Have you learned anything new?"

I explained that it appeared a toxin found in certain types of sea creatures might be the cause of Cole's death. I reiterated that it was my opinion that the missing glass had something to do with the murder. The toxin may have been delivered in the drink, but no one could find the glass or the redhead I spoke to, which was odd.

"You said the redhead was at the scene. Where did she come from?"

"I'm not sure. She was just someone in the crowd standing around the body. She said she'd been there most of the day and had seen a woman bring the drink to Cole, but according to Colin, no one remembered seeing her."

"Colin?"

"One of the HPD on the scene."

Luke sat back in his chair. I liked the fact that I had his full attention. Having someone's full attention was a lot rarer than you might think it would be.

"So where did she go after you finished speaking to her?"

I thought about it. I tried to remember whether I'd seen her walk away, but I really wasn't certain.

"I'm not sure. We were talking when Kekoa ran up. I turned my attention to her, and Jason and his team arrived shortly afterward. I wanted to get a look at Cole's room before anyone else had the opportunity, so we left. I never did turn back to look for the redhead again. I suppose she was still standing there when I left."

Luke didn't even flinch when I mentioned sneaking into Cole's room. There was no doubt about it; I was beginning to like this guy more and more as I got to know him.

"Do you think she could be the one who took the glass?" Luke asked.

"I don't know. I suppose anyone who was there could have taken it."

"You said Jason and his team had just arrived when you left. What would you say the time lapse was between you leaving the vicinity of the body and Jason arriving on the beach?"

"Not long. Maybe a minute at the most."

"So the glass was on the table one minute and gone the next. The person who took it had to have been right there."

Suddenly I wanted very much to figure out who the woman with the curly red hair was and how she might or might not have been involved in my mystery.

"There must be someone on the beach who saw the woman. I'm working tomorrow. I'll be sure Mitch assigns me to tower two again so I can ask around. A lot of the locals who frequent that beach are there almost every day. The woman was actually very striking with all that red hair. Someone must know who she is."

"I'm sure someone does. Don't worry; we'll figure this out."

I smiled at Luke. He really seemed to be going out of his way to be supportive and helpful. I'm not sure why I'd never noticed how intelligent he was. Probably because I'd made it my mission in life to avoid him.

"Would you like another sandwich?" Luke asked after I'd cleaned my plate.

"No, thank you. I'm stuffed. It was really delicious. Ono is my favorite fish."

"Mine as well. If you're finished eating would you like to meet Lucifer?"

"I am. And then maybe you can show me around before we have to head to the Jungle."

"The jungle?"

"It's a bar. I'll explain while we walk."

Chapter 4

Lucifer was absolutely the most adorable baby of any kind I'd ever seen. He was pure black with huge eyes and seemed to like me from the moment we met. I had a feeling a beautiful friendship was in the making, even if he was a horse who would someday grow to an enormous, life-threatening size.

"He's so cute." I hung over the railing of the corral, watching Lucifer interact with his mother. "Much too cute to be named Lucifer."

"He won't be cute for long. His father is enormous and I'm hoping Lucifer will be as well. As for the name, I had a black stallion named Lucifer when I was a child. He was probably my favorite of all the horses in my life. I guess I have a fondness for the name."

"It's so weird to think of you as a kid. Do you have siblings?"

"Two older brothers and two older sisters."

I smiled as Lucifer began to nurse. "So you're the baby of the family?"

Luke nodded. "To be honest, it's a designation I still find myself trying to overcome."

"I get that. My brothers think it's their duty to coddle and protect me. It's like having six overprotective fathers instead of just one. I think the fact that my number still hasn't come up for the police academy might be directly related to interference from the J team."

"The J team?"

I explained about the name thing and the tendency of all my brothers to treat me like I was some sort of fragile flower. Although I had no proof, and there were admittedly other factors such as my size and tendency to get into trouble that might also be working against me, I suspected one or more of my brothers has used their influence to ensure that my name remained firmly at the bottom of the list.

"Wow, that's rough," Luke sympathized. "I guess I was coddled when I was young, but since I've become an adult I feel like I've earned the respect of my siblings. At least most of the time. Though none of them understand why I wanted to move to New York and they really didn't get why I would want to live in Hawaii. There's even been talk among some family members of an intervention."

I laughed. "Do they all still live in Texas?"

"Not only do they all still live there, they all live within thirty miles of the ranch where we grew up. My oldest brother plans to take over the family ranch when my dad retires, so he still lives on the property, although he does have his own house."

"Is he married?"

"Single."

"And your other brother?"

"My dad helped him buy his own spread just down the road. He's also single, in case you were wondering."

"And your sisters?"

"Both married to ranchers they've known their whole lives."

"So you really were the only one to leave the nest and try new things?"

"Pretty much. Like I said, none of them understand my thinking in the least, but because I support myself and don't depend on financial support from the family, there isn't much any of them can do about it."

I stepped down from my elevated position on one of the crossed boards that made up the corral. "I love my family and really can't imagine not having them in my life, but I do sometimes wonder if they aren't holding me back. Was it hard to make the break and do your own thing?"

Luke paused. "Not really. I guess I never gave it a lot of thought. I just went off to college as was expected of me, and when I graduated I decided to try something other than ranching. I'm not sure my decision to leave Texas had anything to do with my family. At least not on a conscious level. But now that we're talking about it, maybe I did want a chance to prove I could make it on my own."

Suddenly Luke was not only moving from the position of enemy to friend but it seemed as if we might be kindred spirits. This wasn't good. This wasn't good at all. The next thing I knew we'd be surfing together, and maybe grabbing a cold one at the end of the day. There was only one place a relationship like that could lead, and there was no way I was ever going to climb onto the back of a four-legged death machine.

"Do all your brothers work for HPD?"

"No. My second oldest brother Jason just recently made detective for HPD, and my fourth brother Justin is a street cop on the force, but John, Jimmy, and Jeff live on and work for the police departments on other islands. John is the oldest, and he intentionally applied for the Maui PD because he didn't want to work under my dad, who has since retired but was very much active when John was ready to begin his career. I was kind of surprised when Jason stayed on the island because he hasn't always gotten along with our dad, but he married a local girl who wanted to stay close to her family. My third brother, Jimmy, lives and works on Kaui, and my youngest brother, Jeff, works on the Maui PD with John." I felt myself blushing. "I really don't know why I'm telling you all this."

"Because we're getting to know each other and I asked?"

"Yeah, I guess. I think you'd like my brothers. They make me nuts at times, but they're all good guys. They'll all be at my parents' house on Sunday. You should stop by."

Yikes. Did I really just invite Luke to attend a family dinner?

"I'd like that. There's a buyer for one of my mares coming by in the morning to take a second look at her, but if it works out I'd like to meet your family."

I shrugged. Best to play it cool. "Yeah. Whatever. I can text you the address. Which mare are you selling?"

"The little blond mustang that was in the pasture when you first entered the drive. The buyer lives on the island and is looking for a gentle mare for his daughter. I think Honey will be perfect."

"Is that what you're doing up here? Breeding stock to sell?"

"Not really. At least not at this point. The man who's interested in Honey is a friend of sorts, and I wanted to help match his daughter with the perfect horse, so I offered to sell Honey to him if the daughter liked her once she met her. When I was looking for someone to breed Halo to—that's Lucifer's mother—I realized how challenging it can be to find just the right pairing. If this works out like I hope it will I might try it again, so I suppose there will come a point when I'll have to sell off some of my stock to make room for others."

"At least you have a lot of room to work with."

"I do. Would you like to see the house?"

The house was gorgeous. When you entered there were hallways to both your right and left that led, I assumed, to other wings of the huge home. If you continued straight the space opened up to a great room with a wall of windows looking out over the sea. The great room was a huge area that would accommodate quite a large party. To the left of it was a large kitchen, which I'd seen when I'd been to the house with Brody, and a large dining area.

Each of the hallways seemed to branch into another. I was pretty sure I'd get lost in the maze should I ever have the chance to be in the house alone. When I'd visited it with Brody we'd come in off the patio through the kitchen door. I'd seen the great room from the kitchen but hadn't had the opportunity to view the rest of the house.

"It's really an amazing place."

"Thank you. I've put a lot of work into it. It was pretty run-down when I bought it, but I knew finding such a large piece of land wasn't going to be easy, so I decided to take on the fixer-upper rather than looking for the perfect house." Luke looked at his watch. "What time was Branson supposed to meet his contact at the bar?"

"Four. I guess we should go. I'm not sure if the person he was set to meet knows he's dead and therefore won't show up, or if the news hasn't carried that far inland yet."

"How are we going to figure out who he was supposed to meet even if he or she does show up?"

"I have no idea."

"We'll take my truck, and then I'll bring you back here afterward to get your Jeep."

"What about Sandy?"

"He'll be fine hanging out here with Duke and Dallas."

The drive inland was beautiful. Although I've lived on this island my entire life, the beauty never ceases to cause me to catch my breath and give thanks for the majesty surrounding me.

The Jungle Bar can only be reached by turning off the highway onto a narrow road that feeds into a dirt drive. The bar is strictly a locals' establishment where any visitors who might stumble on to the place are quickly made aware they aren't welcome. The place itself looks like nothing more than a frond-covered hut from the outside, but inside it's warm and welcoming in a rustic sort of way. Luke and I arrived with fifteen minutes to spare. We ordered drinks and took a seat in the corner, away from the spotlight but in a good position to see everyone who entered or exited the establishment.

Although it was early, there were already quite a few patrons: all men, some shooting the breeze and some shooting pool. There was live music at night, performed by local musicians, and although the place was well off the beaten path it tended to attract a steady clientele. Still, I was surprised to see so many customers so early in the day. I'd dated a guy for a while who loved this place, so although it had been some time since I'd dropped in, I knew the bartender and wasn't considered to be an outsider. Luke and I spoke quietly so as not to be overheard, but we really didn't want to attract attention.

"Any idea what we're looking for?" Luke asked.

"Something that doesn't fit."

Given the fact that the Jungle catered to locals and locals only, Luke was one of the few haoles on the premises, yet no one seemed to care that he was there. There were a few transplants who had earned membership rights in the unofficial club, but more often than not they were accompanied by people with Hawaiian blood, like me.

After we'd been at the bar for about fifteen minutes a beautiful woman with dark hair and light skin walked in alone. She headed straight for the bar, where she said something to the bartender that I couldn't quite make out before making her way to a table at the back of the room. The woman was stunning, and although she looked somewhat out of place, no one paid her any attention, which told me this wasn't her first visit to the establishment. She sat down across from a man of Japanese descent who had been sitting alone. He looked vaguely familiar, but I couldn't quite place him. Still, I was certain I'd seen him before.

I watched as the woman said something to him, then took a thumb drive from her cleavage and handed it to him. He inserted the drive into a small handheld device. He paused for several seconds while I assumed he waited to see something specific occur on his screen; then he put the device and thumb drive in his pocket, stood up, and left the bar. The woman waited approximately two minutes before standing up and walking out as well. I used my phone to take a quick photo of her while pretending to check my messages.

"Should we follow her?" Luke asked after the woman walked out the door.

"No. Let's have another drink."

"Another drink?"

"The man standing in the corner with a pool stick but not playing pool is watching the other patrons. It's my guess he's watching to see if anyone follows either the man or the woman. I don't come here a lot, but I do come often enough that my presence isn't suspect, in spite of the fact that I'm from a cop family. But if we get up now we may as well announce our real reason for being here."

Luke actually looked impressed by my logic. "Another rum?"

"Make it a double," I answered. "A little karaoke should dispel anyone's suspicions as to our real reason for being here."

"You sing karaoke?"

"I've been known to after a few shots. I'm actually somewhat famous for it around these parts. Don't get me wrong: I'm terrible. But an off-key rendition of some currently popular song will dispel any doubts that anyone who was placed here as a lookout may have as to my reason for being here."

After two more rounds and three really bad songs, Luke and I left and headed back toward his ranch. The fact that I'd stopped singing a good fifteen minutes earlier and Luke was still laughing went a long way toward dispelling the warm and fuzzy feeling I'd found myself beginning to develop toward him.

"It wasn't that bad," I defended myself.

"Oh, yeah. It really was. At one point you sounded exactly like a cat on a hot tin roof."

"Very funny. I wasn't trying to be good. I wanted everyone to think I was a lot drunker than I was. I have no idea who the woman was, and although the man looked familiar, I couldn't place him. I have a bad feeling about whatever it was that just went down."

"Do you think maybe we should fill your brother in on all this?"

"Maybe," I admitted. "Let's see if we can figure out the identity of the woman in the bar and then decide for sure."

"We can Google Branson. Maybe he was seen in public with her at some point and a photo will identify her by name."

It was a long shot, but at this point it was the only lead we had.

When we returned to the ranch Luke made us salads with fresh greens and ahi tuna. We took our light meal out onto the patio, where he had set up electrical wiring to be used specifically with his computer and other electronic equipment. The patio area had its own source of high-speed Internet, creating an outdoor office of sorts that ran the equipment as efficiently as the office inside his home.

After we ate Luke logged onto his computer and began to surf the Web. Unsurprisingly, there were quite a few photos of Cole; he was an aggressive businessman and investor who had a long history of spearheading large projects. If there was a photo of him with the woman we'd seen in the bar, locating it could very well be like finding a needle in a haystack.

I remembered the redheaded woman saying a beautiful brunette with fair skin had brought the drink to Cole on the beach. The woman in the bar was certainly beautiful, and she was a brunette. Could she be the same one?

I looked over Luke's shoulder as he worked. At one point I recognized someone in a crowd. I pointed to the screen where the photo was displayed. "See that guy sitting in the back of the room?"

"The guy with the green shirt?"

"Yeah. I've seen him before somewhere. Do you know his name?"

"No. Why?"

I tried to remember where I'd seen the man. I really didn't go a lot of places, so chances were it had been at the resort. The more I thought about it the more certain I was he was a semiregular guest. "I'll need to confirm it with Kekoa, but I think that's Patrick Anderson. He visits the resort almost every year. I didn't put it together before, but I seem to remember Kekoa mentioning that he works as a planner for one of those big corporations with resorts all over the world. If he was photographed in the same room with Branson Cole maybe Patrick is the Anderson in Cole, Anderson, and Devlin."

"I guess that makes sense. I suppose if Branson and Anderson were both interested in developing land in the area it makes sense they would both have visited and might have made a connection and decided to go into business together."

"Can you print a photo of each man?"

"Yeah. Are you going to look into it further?"

"I am. I should probably get going now, but if you ever do find a photo of the woman we saw at the bar let me know. I have the photo I took with my phone, but finding her in some sort of context would help us identify her."

"Are you going to talk to your brother about the meeting in the bar?"

"I'm not sure. If I tell him what I saw and how I saw it, he'll probably figure out some way to put me under house arrest for my own safety. I think I'll wait to see if we come up with something on our own."

I rounded up Sandy and headed back to the condo. When I got there both Cam and Kekoa were out, so I grabbed my laptop and headed out onto the lanai. It was a warm evening with a gentle breeze and the thought of trying to work in the hot condo wasn't appealing. I couldn't help but notice Mr. B was home. Kekoa doesn't think there's anything odd going on with our neighbor beyond the fact that he likes his privacy, but I still have my doubts.

I Googled both Patrick Anderson and Branson Cole. Anderson was a lead planner at World Resort Corporation. The guy wasn't one to enjoy the water or the beach during his stays with us, so I didn't know him all that well, but I was sure Kekoa had chatted with him from time to time, so maybe she would know whether or not he was the Anderson in business with Cole, as I suspected.

Branson Cole dealt with many types of investments, but it seemed his specialty was finding backers for whatever company he was currently involved with. It made sense that he and Anderson would team up if there was interest in building a resort here on the island. Anderson had the background to plan and oversee the construction and Cole had the contacts to fund the project.

Which left Devlin. I didn't have a first name, which made it pretty much impossible to find the guy. I thought it odd that CAD Development didn't have some sort of flashy Web page with photos and bios of all three men. If they were trying to attract investors, as Luke indicated they were, it would seem a spectacular Web site would be a must. All I'd been able to find was a single-page site with the company's logo and an architect's rendering of the completed resort. There was an e-mail address, but I couldn't find any other contact information—not an address or even a phone number. The whole thing was beyond weird as far as I was concerned.

I pulled up all the photos I could find of Branson Cole. Luke had said he was seeing a woman named Helena who lived on the island. Maybe if I could find her, I'd find the answers I was looking for.

I was trying to decide whether or not to head inside when Kekoa arrived. She asked what I was doing and I filled her in.

"I don't know a lot about Mr. Anderson," Kekoa said after I asked her just that question. "We always chat for a few minutes when he's checking in or out; I ask him what project he's working on and where he's traveled since the last time he stayed with us. Our conversations are pretty superficial and brief. You might talk to Kimo, though. I think Mr. Anderson spends quite a bit of time in the bar when he's staying with us, and you know how people tend to talk to bartenders."

"Yeah, that's a good idea. I'll talk to him tomorrow. So how was dinner with your parents?"

"Tense."

"They still fighting?"

Kekoa sighed. "More than ever. I really am beginning to suspect they might split up once Halina graduates high school in a few months."

Unlike me, who's the youngest in the family, Kekoa is the oldest. She has two sisters: Molina, who's in college on the mainland, and Halina, who's a senior in high school.

"Maybe once Halina graduates and they have some time to themselves they'll work things out," I offered, although I really didn't believe that. Kekoa's parents fought more than any couple I'd ever known.

"I doubt it. To be honest, I think it might be better for everyone if they did part. I find myself avoiding them so I won't be put in the position of taking sides. I know Halina feels the same way. Like Molina, she plans to go to college on the mainland, and she's made several references to the fact that she doesn't plan to return to the islands after she graduates."

I felt sorry for Kekoa. I knew her relationship with her sisters was important to her. My brothers made me nuts, but at least they were around to ruin my life. If Halina left too, Kekoa would be alone on the island. Well, not alone. She'd still have me and the other million or so people who live here, but you get what I mean.

"What's your schedule for the next few weeks?" Kekoa asked.

"I'm on Tuesday, Wednesday, Friday, and Saturday for the next few months. Why?"

"I was hoping we'd have a day off together. I'd love to go shopping, but I'm on Sunday through Thursday for the next few weeks at least. Maybe I'll take one of my vacation days on a Monday or Thursday."

"Sounds like fun. I've been wanting to get some new shoes and the selection is a lot better on the south shore. We could do lunch at that place near the beach we ate at last time we were over there. Thursdays are usually best for me because I take Elva to bingo on Mondays. Why don't you wait until I get this case solved? I'd hate to have you take a vacation day and then end up bailing on you."

"You really think you can solve this before Jason does?"

"I do and I will."

Chapter 5

Friday, March 11

Do you know what happens to WSOs when it rains? They get wet. Don't get me wrong: I spend half of my life wet, but when the moisture is pelting your body from above it isn't quite the same rush as when it embraces and surrounds you as you slip into its depths.

"Mitch, are you there? It's Lani. Over."

I waited for Mitch to respond to my request to take a break; hopefully an extended one that would last until the torrential downpour that was drenching the island subsided. Not only was it raining but the air temperature had dropped and the wind had picked up quite a bit. In other words, I was not only wet, I was freezing.

"The beach is deserted and the only surfers left in the water are idiots who deserve what they get for trying to surf in a hurricane. Mitch? Can you read me?"

Chances were the radio had gotten enough water in it to short something out. I knew I was supposed to wait to be relieved from my post, but enough was enough. I put out the sign that indicated there was no WSO on duty, grabbed my backpack, and headed for the main office. With any luck Mitch would be around and I could take my break and get dried off.

"You look like a drowned rat," Drake commented when I walked into the covered building.

"Where's Mitch?"

"On a break."

"A break?" I screeched. "I'm getting pelted out there and the guy can't be bothered to call me in before heading out on his break?"

"Oh, yeah. I guess I was supposed to radio everyone to let them know to come in and wait out the storm. You were the last one on my list and I guess I forgot."

I shot Drake a dirty look. Forgot my ass. There was no doubt in my mind that the idiot had left me out there on purpose. I wanted to express my rage, but the last time I'd done that I was the one who ended up with a suspension without pay. I simply turned and headed toward the locker room. There were some fights that weren't worth having.

Once I'd taken a warm shower, dried off, and changed into shorts and a sweatshirt, I was feeling much better. I decided now was as good a time as any to talk to Kimo. It was early in the day, so hopefully the bar wouldn't be crowded despite the rain. According to the schedule Kimo would be in the open-air beach bar, which was covered on the top but open on the sides. Unless the wind was blowing hard enough to affect the sheltered portion, the interior of the drinking establishment would be nice and dry.

I hurried through the rain to find a few patrons taking refuge inside the hut-shaped room, but not so many as to prevent Kimo and me from having a conversation.

"What can I getcha?" Kimo asked.

"Just water. I'm still on duty until someone tells me otherwise."

"Heard the rain and wind is supposed to continue through the night. I'm kind of surprised Mitch hasn't sent you home."

"He wasn't in the office when I checked in. Drake said something about a break, but it seems an odd time to take one, so I'm thinking something else is up. Anyway, I'm here to ask you about Patrick Anderson."

"What about him?"

"Did you know he was part of the company that wants to build the resort around the bend along with Branson Cole and some guy named Devlin?"

"Pat might have mentioned it. Why do you ask?"

"I was just curious, given the fact that Mr. Cole died on our beach a few days ago under mysterious circumstances."

"Thought the old guy had a heart attack."

"Yeah, maybe. So what can you tell me about Anderson?"

Kimo shrugged. "Not much to tell. The man spent a lifetime working for another development company. A year or so ago, maybe less, someone named Devlin approached Pat and asked if he would be interested in teaming up to build a resort on the land down the beach. Of course Pat was interested. From what he said, designing his own resort had been a dream of his. Pat didn't have a lot of money, but Devlin said they'd bring in a third partner with connections to wealthy investors."

"That must have been Branson Cole."

"Yeah, I guess."

"So other than coming up with the idea, do you know what Devlin brought to the deal?"

"Relationships. According to Pat, Devlin knew the owner of the land where they wanted to build, and it was through that relationship that they were able to work out a deal. At least that's what I was told."

Okay, so Devlin had the idea and the relationships, Anderson had the knowhow to plan and build a resort, and Cole had the resources and connections to get the money. Made sense. What didn't make sense was how this could have gotten Cole killed.

"I heard the project might be in trouble. It seems there's a group of environmentalists that wants to block it."

Kimo refilled my water. "Pat mentioned that was a risk. In fact, the environmentalists created problems in a lot of the places the resort he worked for built. He said the issues usually work themselves out, so he wasn't too worried about it."

"When was the last time you saw Anderson?"

"Guess about a month ago. He was here with a woman. A real looker."

I showed Kimo the photo of the woman in the bar. "That her?"

"Yep, looks like."

"Do you know her name?"

"Nope."

I wasn't sure my conversation with Kimo had brought me any new information, but I supposed it did verify what I already suspected.

"Were you working in this bar on Wednesday?"

Kimo nodded.

"Do you remember selling a rum punch to Cole, or maybe to an attractive dark-haired woman who might have delivered the drink to him?"

"I sold a lot of rum punches on Wednesday but none to Cole. At least not directly. I do know he wasn't much of a drinker. In fact, he was in here the day before he was found on the beach and ordered a soft drink. I tried to talk him into one of our signature drinks, but he said something about a heart condition and needing to watch his alcohol intake."

Okay, that was odd. Based on the evidence left near Cole's chair, it had looked like he'd drunk the potent drink. As usual, something wasn't adding up.

Mitch had returned by the time I returned to the command headquarters. He informed me that he was releasing all of us for the remainder of the day and told me to call in before heading in to work in the morning if the storm hadn't passed. It sounded like we were in for a big one. While it was raining hard the wind wasn't really all that bad but, according to Mitch, that was supposed to change over the next few hours.

When I got home Cam and Kekoa were sitting at the dining table playing a card game. The rain was coming down in sheets and, as predicted, the wind had started to pick up and was hitting the side of the condo with enough velocity to cause the building to shake.

"I'm surprised to find you both home. I sort of figured you'd be out because you're both off tomorrow."

"Cam is sulking because Makena has a date with the new surfing instructor and I decided my brief relationship with Don had come to its natural conclusion."

"I'm not sulking," Cam defended himself.

"He's sulking."

"Makena and I aren't exclusive. She can date whatever moron she chooses."

Kekoa discarded a two of spades which made Cam curse. Yup, there was no doubt about it; Cam was sulking.

I bent down to greet Sandy, then looked out the open window at the pouring rain. "I'm going to check on Elva before I get settled in."

"Actually, Sean was by earlier and invited everyone down to their place for dinner," Kekoa informed me. "The guys just got back from Mexico, so we're doing Mexican food. Kevin is making a huge pot of his homemade chili verde, Carina is bringing tamales, and Elva is bringing dessert."

"So what are we bringing?"

Cam held up a bag of tortilla chips and a carton of salsa.

"I made guacamole as well," Kekoa added.

With the exception of Mr. B in unit 6, the tenants of the Shell Beach Condominiums are like a big family. Kevin Green and Sean Trainor lived in unit 5, which has the largest living area of all the condos. Sean and Kevin were flight attendants who were rarely home, but when they were on the island, they were always the first to organize a party. The fact that we were experiencing a near hurricane and they chose to serve the rum-and-fruit-based drink by the same name was typical of the fun the couple often initiated.

Carina West lived in unit 4 and was a dancer at a local luau. She's a year younger than I am but has a heart the size of someone who has experienced a lot in life. So far I haven't been able to crack the façade she presents to the world to find the tragedy I'm certain serves as the foundation for her approach to life. Carina worked nights and wasn't around a lot in the evenings, but when she was, she could usually be found watching old movies with Elva in unit 2.

Unit 3 was open but if Elva was correct would soon be occupied by a young mother and her adopted daughter. It remained to be seen how they'd fit into our little family, but Elva had said she'd picked up a good vibe from them, and she was rarely wrong.

I changed and we grabbed the chips, salsa, and guacamole and headed down the sidewalk to unit 5. Sean and Kevin had done a lot better job making their space into a home than Cam, Kekoa, and me. Our condo is decorated in a theme I think of as yard sale hodgepodge, whereas Sean and Kevin have brought the sand and sea into their space by decorating in varying shades of blue, gray, and white. Our furniture is secondhand, while the guys in unit 5 have purchased the finest furniture and electronics money can buy.

"To rainy nights and good friends to help pass the time." Kevin held up his glass in a toast.

"Hear, hear," everyone responded.

Carina sat on the floor petting Sandy while Kekoa chatted with Elva and Cam helped Kevin in the kitchen. The music had been turned up in order to be heard over the sound of the waves crashing onto the beach, making carrying on a conversation difficult at best. I love it when everyone comes together for a spontaneous meal at the end of the day. Sean and Kevin are the most likely to host such an event, but there are times when Carina and I will bring food over to Elva's for the three of us to share when Cam and Kekoa are out.

"I feel a little bad we're all here except for Mr. B. Should we invite him to come over?" I wondered.

"I tried," Kevin reported. "I knocked on the door and waited, but he never answered."

"His lights and television are on."

"They were when I knocked as well," Kevin informed me. "I suppose he could have been in the shower."

"Or he's just avoiding us," Cam offered.

"I'm sure he'll be over to complain about the noise," Sean commented. "We can invite him to join us then."

I sat on one of the barstools and watched Sean mix a pitcher of potent drinks. He was a fit man of average build and a snappy dresser, kindhearted, with a pleasant disposition and an appreciation for art and the theater. He was friendly and neatly groomed, and I've heard he was an excellent flight attendant. I know he made a decent amount of money and had been pretty much everywhere he'd ever wanted to go, but I often wondered whether his talent would have been better served if he'd gone into fashion or interior design.

Kevin, on the other hand, reminded me of Cam. A large man who enjoyed cooking and sports of all kinds, he tended to dress casually, and while Sean enjoyed the opera, Kevin was more of a heavy metal type of guy. On the surface they seemed as different as two men could be, but they seemed to have what it took to sustain a relationship that would go the distance.

"So how was Mexico?" I asked Sean.

"Hot, muggy, and overcast. The surfing wasn't what we hoped and it was too hot to do much hiking, but the food was good and we enjoyed the amenities at the resort."

When he'd heard about their wedding, Sean and Kevin had been given a two-week stay at a luxury resort by one of the frequent fliers who patronized the airline they worked for. They'd just returned home earlier that day.

"It was really nice of Mr. Brown to comp your stay."

"The guy's loaded. The resort in Mexico is only one of the ones he owns."

"He owns the resort? I thought he just worked there."

"No, he owns it. At least partially. I think there are several partners and a handful of investors with their hand in the pot. Speaking of investors, I heard about Mr. Cole. It's a shame what happened."

"You knew him?"

"As much as one can know a customer. I usually work the first-class cabin and Cole always flew first class. In fact, he was on the last flight I worked before Kevin and I headed for Mexico."

"Which was two weeks ago."

"Yeah, thereabout. Sixteen days ago, to be specific. Why?"

"He only checked into the Dolphin Bay on Sunday."

"He mentioned he had plans to stay with a woman he knew on the island. I imagine he must have done that first. Did you know he was planning to develop his own resort on the island?"

"I heard that. It seems he had a couple of partners and planned to develop the land east of Dolphin Bay."

"Cole seemed genuinely excited about the project, but Mr. Brown, the customer who comped Kevin and me in Mexico, told me that he thought the whole thing was a scam."

I frowned. "A scam? What do you mean by that?"

"Brown told me that he'd looked into developing that piece of land himself a while back, but there were a number of issues that prevented it from being a good candidate for such a large project. He said any developer worth their salt would have pulled the history of the property prior to buying it and would have known that project wasn't going anywhere. It was Brown's opinion that Cole used the project to scam his investors out of their money."

If that was true it certainly provided a motive for someone to kill the man. The question was, who were the investors and which of them killed him?

I was contemplating the idea of calling Luke and asking him to make a run at his father again in the hope of learning the identity of at least some of the investors when a thundering sound shook the whole building.

"What was that?" Elva cried.

I looked out the window. The rain was still coming down hard, the surf had increased in height, and the wind seemed to be pounding everything in its path.

"Looks like one of those big palms near the water fell," I answered.

"Do you think we're safe here?" Elva asked.

I really wasn't sure, but I knew trying to drive in this mess wasn't a good idea. "I think we're fine. I'm going to go check on Mr. B. He might be an introvert, but it seems like even an introvert would prefer not to be alone on a night like this."

"I'll go with you," Sean offered.

Sean pulled waterproof jackets out of his hall closet for each of us. Personally I was fine with getting rained on, but I could see why Sean didn't want to ruin his new shirt, which looked like silk. It only took a few seconds to walk from one unit to the next, but even a little bit of rain wouldn't be good for the expensive fabric.

I knocked hard on the door to unit 6 and waited. No answer. I knocked again and called Mr. B's name. Still no answer. "I hope he's okay."

Sean pulled something that looked sort of like a Swiss Army knife out of his pocket. "I can get in. We should check on him. There's no way he's sleeping through all this ruckus."

"You're going to pick the lock?"

"Funny but true story: My dad was a thief. A good one too."

"You're kidding."

"'Fraid not. He taught me everything he knew before he passed on a few years ago."

"And your mom?"

"They met when she tried to pick his pocket."

I laughed. "Are you pulling my leg?"

"Would I do that?"

He would, but I had the sense he wasn't. What were the odds that a member of a family of cops would be such good friends with a member of a family of thieves?

The door opened easily once Sean had worked his magic and we stepped inside.

"Hello," I called. "Mr. B, are you here? It's Lani, from unit 1. I wanted to make sure you were okay."

My announcement was met with silence. Unlike my condo, which was bright, messy, and lived-in, Mr. B's was stark and devoid of personal items of any kind. The room reminded me of a hotel room, a place of temporary lodging but certainly not a home.

"The place looks deserted," Sean observed.

He was right. I had to wonder why the television was blaring and all the lights were on. I quickly looked through the rooms of the one-bedroom condo just to make sure. The place was completely deserted.

"I'm tempted to turn everything off so it doesn't run all night, but I don't want to give away the fact that we were here," I commented.

"It won't run all night," Sean answered. "Look here. The lights and television are on a timer."

"A timer? That means Mr. B might not have been home all the nights we thought he was just being antisocial."

"Could be. I've never even seen the guy. Have you?"

"No. I haven't ever seen him. I wonder if any of the others have."

The unit had been empty until a month before, when I first noticed the lights. I'd asked Elva, who was always around, who had moved in, and she'd said it was a man named Mr. B. I'd seen the lights go on and off every night, but I'd never had occasion to actually knock on the man's door.

We locked the door behind us and returned to Sean and Kevin's condo. After posing the question to the group, it was determined that no one other than Elva had ever so much as caught a glimpse of Mr. B. She reported that she'd seen him pass by her window on the day he moved in, and then she saw him again on Wednesday, the night the condo was dark. We'd all heard the television and seen the lights go on and off; we'd just assumed he was holed up in his condo, but had he been?

"Okay, it's crazy to think there hasn't been anyone living in the condo," Kekoa insisted. "It seems like there would be signs if the condo was really empty."

"Like what?" I asked.

"I don't know. The mail would pile up or something."

"Not if he didn't have mail delivered to this address," I pointed out. "A lot of people have post office boxes."

"These condos aren't cheap. Why would anyone rent one they weren't going to live in?" Carina asked. "It makes no sense."

I turned to Elva. "You said you saw a man the day Mr. B moved in. What did he look like?"

"He was short. Thin. Had on dark clothes. It was dark and I only saw him from the back, but I'm sure he was no taller than Chen."

Mr. Chen was our landlord.

"So how, if you didn't talk to him, did you know his name was Mr. B?" I wondered.

"I asked Mr. Chen about him when I paid my rent. He said the new tenant had wired the money to rent the apartment, so he hadn't actually spoken to him in person. He said he had a name that was hard to pronounce, so he'd just been referring to him as Mr. B."

English was Mr. Chen's second language and he seemed to find a lot of common words hard to pronounce, so this totally made sense. "Okay, so did you get a better look at him on Wednesday when he passed by your window on the way out?"

"He had a pair of sweats on. Gray. With a hooded sweatshirt. The hood was pulled over his head and he had on dark glasses, so I didn't get a good look."

"So you saw some guy from the back a month or so ago. He lets himself into unit 6, so you ask Mr. Chen who it is and he tells you the man has a hard name to pronounce so he just calls him Mr. B. We all see his lights and television going on and off, but none of us has ever seen *him* until Elva saw him again on Wednesday. What are the odds of that happening?"

"Sean and I are hardly ever here," Kevin reminded me. "At least not during the past month. We were assigned to a European flight and then we were away on our trip. In fact, I bet this is only the fourth or fifth night we've spent in the condo since the man moved in."

Kevin had a point. They had been away a lot lately.

"And I work nights and sleep in late," Carina added. "I figured the guy just came and went when I was either asleep or working."

Cam, Kekoa, and I all agreed that we'd thought it odd that we'd never seen him, but we really hadn't thought much about it. We lived busy lives and figured we'd just missed someone who obviously preferred to keep to himself.

"I think one of us should have a chat with Mr. Chen to see if we can get more information about the guy," I suggested.

"Mr. Chen has left on his trip to visit his family," Elva reminded us. "He won't be back for a month."

"Oh, yeah, I forgot. Okay, I guess we should just all keep an eye on the condo. If anyone sees the guy we should attempt to speak to him. Maybe this whole thing is nothing. The timer could just be a method of dissuading vandals from breaking in when the man is away. Just because he wasn't home tonight doesn't mean he's never been home during the month he's lived here."

"That's true," Sean agreed. "Who's up for another hurricane?"

Everyone agreed the drink made dealing with the weather system by the same name a whole lot easier. Not that we were actually experiencing a hurricane. When I'd checked the Weather Channel they were referring to it as nothing more than a strong storm system, but from where I was sitting it felt like a hurricane.

I couldn't help but think of Luke and all his horses. I guess he must bring them inside when it rained. I hadn't actually counted the stalls in the barn, but it seemed there were enough for every horse and then some. I was thinking that perhaps I should call Luke just to check in when the lights flickered off.

"I have candles and LED lights," Sean assured us.

"And the food is ready," Kevin added.

The newlyweds certainly were prepared for whatever the night might bring. Without the music to drown out the wind and the waves, it sounded like a locomotive was about to plow through the building. I found I was glad I was sharing a meal with friends who felt like family and cared about one another enough to share food and offer comfort during a storm.

Chapter 6

Sunday, March 13

Yesterday had been as quiet as the previous couple of days had been eventful. The storm had blown out as quickly as it had blown in. The sun shone high in the sky, the surf was awesome, and the beach was as busy as I had seen it in quite some time. I executed seven successful rescues and stayed two hours past the end of my shift, and by the time I returned to the condo, I was exhausted and went straight to bed.

Luckily, I wasn't expected at my parents' house until noon today. Cam and Kekoa both had shifts and left before I even got up. If it wasn't for the fact that Sandy was tired of waiting to go out and decided it was time to pounce on me, I might have slept straight through the day.

"Okay, I'm coming." I yawned as Sandy put his face on the mattress next to mine.

He trotted across the room, rummaged through the pile of clothes I'd left on the floor the previous evening, and brought me a shoe in an effort, I assumed, to hurry me along. I crawled out of bed, pulled on some shorts and a clean T-shirt, made the bed, and cleaned up my half of the room, then headed into the kitchen to pour myself a cup of the coffee Kekoa had left in the pot. I searched through the cupboard for something to eat, grabbed a granola bar, and headed out onto the lanai with Sandy.

I hadn't spoken to Luke since Thursday and I wondered if he actually was going to show up for our family dinner. I'd texted him the address and he'd texted back a thank you but never really committed one way or the other. To be honest, I wasn't sure I wanted him to come. Inviting him had been a momentary impulse, but since then I'd given way too much thought to whether or not he'd actually come. On one hand, there was a dark and secret part of my soul that missed his smile and hoped he'd show up, but there was a whole other part of me that knew that falling for Luke wouldn't lead to anything but heartache.

"Beautiful morning," Elva greeted me as she joined me on the lanai and began picking dead buds from the colorful flowers she'd planted in clay pots the previous summer.

"It really is. I sort of wish I could just head to the beach."

"Dinner with the folks?"

"Yeah. It'll be nice to see my brothers, but the waves certainly are calling."

Elva filled a watering can from the hose used to keep the small lawn that fronted the building moist during the periods when the island went too long without rain. "Been a while since all the Pope offspring have shared a meal together, huh?"

"Yeah. I guess the last time was Christmas. Although the brothers all live within a short plane ride, it's hard for everyone to get off work at the same time."

Elva tipped the watering can into the first pot. "I guess working in law enforcement does tend to wreak havoc with work schedules. Is Jeff still on graveyards?"

"He is, but he put in for a couple of vacation days."

"That's nice."

I'd taken Elva with me to my parents' house on several occasions when I knew she'd be alone. The most recent time was the previous Thanksgiving, when all the Popes were in attendance except Jeff, who, as the low man on the totem pole, was scheduled to work. I think Elva got a kick out of the fact that there were so many people in my life and frequently asked about my brothers.

"Looks like Sandy is enjoying the sunshine this morning," Elva commented as she completed her task and sat down on one of the patio chairs next to me.

I watched as Sandy ran back and forth across the beach, chasing the waves as if they existed solely for his entertainment. "I worked a long day yesterday so he didn't get his usual run in the evening." There was something magical about mornings like this one that made everything seem fresh and new. "Did Mr. B ever show up?"

"Not that I saw. The lights came on as usual, but there was no sign that he was back. I've been watching. Now that we know about the timer I've been questioning just how much time the man actually spends at the condo."

"Yeah, the whole thing is really odd. Did Sean and Kevin leave?"

"Yesterday afternoon. They said they're off to Paris and then on to London. They said they'd be home in a week."

I wondered what it would be like to travel the world. I supposed I'd enjoy having new experiences and seeing new sights, but I knew I'd miss the islands after only a short time away. There's something about the tropical breeze, the hibiscus-scented air, and the white sand beaches contrasting with the deep blue sea that beckons me back whenever I venture away for more than a few days.

"I thought we should plan a get-together down on the beach when they get back. Between their work schedules and their impromptu honeymoon, we really never did have much of a chance to celebrate their wedding. It would be fun to throw them a party."

"That sounds lovely. It'll give them a chance to bond with Mary and Malia."

"Did they move in yesterday?"

"Yes," Elva confirmed. "Or at least they brought the first load of their stuff. I think she said she'd be bringing the rest today. She's a teacher, you know. Second grade."

"Has she lived in Hawaii long?"

"Actually, no. She lived in Oregon until last September, although she told me a friend from college lived on Oahu, so she'd visited the island several times. It seems the friend was killed in a car accident last summer and Mary was granted custody of her ten-year-old daughter, Malia. Malia initially moved to Oregon to be with Mary, but she missed her home, so Mary applied for a teaching position on the island.

They've been staying with friends, but Mary decided it was time for them to make a home of their own. I think you're really going to like Mary. She's open and funny and has a huge heart. And Malia…I can't tell you how excited I am to have a little one nearby."

I don't know that I'd ever seen Elva's face light up the way it did when she referred to Malia. "I look forward to meeting them."

"I think they're going to fit right in with our little family. They arrived before the boys left and it seemed obvious Sean was smitten with Malia. He even promised to paint a mural on the wall of her bedroom when they get back into town. It's a shame they don't plan to have a family. He'd make a wonderful father."

"You never know. Now that they're married, Sean and Kevin could decide to settle down and have kids. Did Carina have an opportunity to meet the new tenants?"

Elva nodded. "She's already begun to teach Malia the hula. I think a child in the building is just what we all need."

I smiled. I already had a large and very close family, so I hadn't necessarily been looking for a second family when Cam, Kekoa, and I moved into the condo, but there wasn't a person in the group I didn't count as a very important part of my life.

"Do you have any plans today?" Elva rarely did, but I felt it polite to ask.

"I think I'm going to start a new afghan. My arthritis has been acting up, so it's been a while since I've crocheted, but Malia saw the one on the back of my sofa and mentioned how she'd love to have one in baby blue for her new room. It might take me a while to finish it, but I'm feeling pretty good today and I can't think of anything I'd rather do."

"That's so nice. I'm sure she'll love it."

"I thought I'd stop by the yarn store tomorrow to pick up a deeper blue for the border if you don't mind stopping."

"I'd be happy to."

Every Monday since Elva had fallen and injured her hip three months earlier, I'd driven her into town for her weekly lunch with friends and bingo at the senior center. Although I was far from a senior myself, the eclectic group of men and women who gathered every week welcomed me with open arms and declared me an honorary member. While my service to Elva was supposed to be a temporary one until the doctor cleared her to drive, I found I enjoyed the weekly gathering and was in no hurry for her to resume driving herself.

Elva and I sat in silence sipping our coffee as we watched the waves forming in the distance and rolling toward the shore, growing in height until that perfect moment when they curled and crashed into the churning sea. After a while Elva's phone rang, so she excused herself and went inside. I knew I should probably head in to get ready for my afternoon, but the sun on my shoulders combined with the sound of the waves almost lulled me back to sleep. In fact, I might very well have nodded off if Sandy hadn't decided he was done playing in the surf and was ready for his breakfast.

The house where I grew up and my parents still lived is inland. I suppose there are advantages to living away from the sea. As the elevation climbs it tends to be cooler, for one thing. For another, it's a lot less crowded and the homes are much more affordable. Like the one Jason and Alana live in, my parents' home is on a large lot with a huge pool and a BBQ area. They like to entertain and do so often, so it's not at all unusual for the smoke from a roasting pig or family BBQ to be seen rising from their property.

"Aunt Lani!" Kale and Kala ran toward me the moment I stepped onto the back patio. Although they're twins, they're very much different in both looks and personality. Kala has her mother's beauty and soulful eyes. She's petite, like I am, and has a tendency to be a thinker in spite of her young age, while Kale is tall and husky like his daddy and has an outgoing personality that's hard to resist.

"Hi, guys. It looks like you've already been in the pool."

"As soon as we got here," Kale informed me. "Uncle Jimmy is swimming with us. You should come."

Jimmy had arrived from Kauai the previous day and planned to stay for a few days.

"Maybe in a bit. Are your mom and dad here?"

"Dad's in the house talking to Tutu Kane [grandfather] about a case Dad is working on and Mom is in the kitchen with Tutu Wahine [grandmother] talking about Uncle Jeff," Kala informed me. "They all shooed us away; they said their conversations weren't for little ears."

"I'll bet. Is Uncle Jeff here yet?"

"No, but he called and talked to Tutu Wahine, and that made her mad. I even heard her say a bad word."

"You guys go ahead and swim with Uncle Jimmy. I'm going to go inside and say hi to everyone, but I'll join you a little later."

I'd openly admitted that I was looking forward to the fireworks Jeff's arrival with Candy would cause, but I secretly hoped for everyone's sake that Jeff would do the smart thing and attend the family event on his own. Though, knowing Jeff, who seems to thrive on chaos and discord, he'd simply called to inform Mom that he planned to bring a date. John lived on Maui as well, so they probably planned to make the trip on the same flight. John tended to be as levelheaded as Jeff was impulsive, so maybe he'd had the opportunity to head Jeff off at the pass and suggest there was a time and place to introduce Candy back into the family and this wasn't it.

Kala had said Jason was talking to my dad, so I decided to sneak into the house to see if I could overhear what was being said. My old bedroom, which now served as a guest room, was directly over my dad's office. I knew from experience that if you listened carefully you could hear what was being discussed from one room to the other. I was lucky not to run into anyone as I quickly scurried up the stairs, went into the bedroom, and closed the door. I lay down on the tile floor and began to listen.

"The toxin that was used is pretty sophisticated," I heard Jason say. "I doubt we're looking at a scorned lover."

"Did you look at the man's activities prior to his stay at the resort?" my dad asked.

"We're in the process of looking into it. So far nothing really stands out as suspect. He arrived on the island sixteen days ago and checked into a motel in Honolulu, where he stayed for three nights. We haven't found a paper trail of his whereabouts between his stays at the motel and the resort. I'm guessing he spent his time at a private residence, but we're still looking."

"Were you able to find anything on his phone that might point to his whereabouts?" Dad continued his questions.

"So far we haven't found a phone. He had nothing with him on the beach. We checked his room and found his wallet but no phone."

"And his business associates?"

"Both Anderson and Devlin seemed to be very upset by Cole's passing. They mentioned that without Cole's backers they were never going to have the funding to pull off the project. I realize they could have been lying, but neither partner was on the island when Cole died."

"One or both of them could have hired someone to administer the toxin."

"True, but I don't really see how either had motive."

I heard a phone ring. Jason answered it, but it sounded like my dad had left the office. I tried to make out what Jason was saying, but he wasn't directly beneath me anymore and was speaking softly. I didn't want to be caught spying, so I quickly left the room and made my way back outside. I figured I'd head over to the pool, and if anyone asked I would say I'd been there the whole time.

Jason had said he didn't know where Cole had been between his three days in Honolulu and checking in to the Dolphin Bay, but I remembered Sean mentioning that Cole had planned to stay with a woman. Maybe Helena? I wasn't sure if that was significant, but it seemed like the woman might be tied in to the murder.

I was halfway to the pool when I decided to stop to say hi to my fourth brother, Justin, who was watching the outdoor television on the covered patio. He worked for HPD and I hoped he'd have additional news on Branson Cole's murder. Jason was the official detective in charge of the case and was unlikely to share anything with me, but Justin was a lot easier-going and therefore more likely to drop a piece of gossip.

"Hey, squirt." Justin pulled me in for a bear-size hug when I sat down next to him. "You're braver than I give you credit for if you're willing to show your face around here today."

"Brave? Why?"

"I heard you've been messing around in Jason's case. He isn't happy about it."

"Messing around? What do you mean, messing around?"

Justin tugged on one of my braids the way he had when we were kids. "Someone found your phone and turned it in to Jason when they realized the significance of the photos you took on it. Lame move."

"Damn." I closed my eyes and hung my head. Jason was going to kill me, if Dad didn't kill me first. "Does Dad know?"

"I don't think so. Jason can be a jerk, but he's still your brother, and we Pope kids look out for one another. I'm fairly certain you can expect a lecture from Jason, but I think your secret is safe as far as Dad is concerned. I think Jason and I are the only two who know about your little B and E escapade."

"I didn't break and enter. I had the key I found near Cole's body."

Justin just raised one eyebrow. "So that's where the key went. We wondered why Cole didn't have it with him."

Interesting. I didn't really take the key, so I also had to wonder why it wasn't in Cole's possession.

"Look, I didn't take anything other than the photos. In fact, I was very careful not to touch anything or leave any evidence behind. I found the body and I was curious. You know how bad I want to be a cop. I figured if I could solve the case before anyone else, the HPD would have to give me the shot we both know I deserve. If I hadn't dropped my phone when I swung out over the balcony I would have been home free."

"You swung out over the balcony?"

I explained about Jason coming in and my need to make a quick escape.

"Look, kid, I get it. I've been living in Jason's shadow ever since I joined the HPD and it gets old. But you aren't *Hawaii Five-0*. You're more like *Hawaii Five Foot-0*. If you keep messing around with this sort of thing you're going to get hurt."

"I'm as capable of figuring this out as you and Jason. I may be short, but I'm smart and I deserve a chance. Maybe if you would all stop blocking my acceptance into the academy I could work with you instead of on my own."

"Hey." Justin raised his hands in the air. "I can't speak for Jason, but I'm not blocking anything. If you want my opinion, it's stunts like this that are keeping you out. The HPD doesn't have a lot of use for someone who acts first and thinks later."

I hated to admit it, but Justin could be right. Maybe I should just apologize for what I'd done and then let the whole thing go.

"Maybe I should just leave," I decided. "I don't want to be responsible for causing a ruckus at Mom's party."

Justin looked toward the house. "I think you're safe. It looks like Jeff has gone and diverted everyone's attention."

"I can't believe Jeff and Candy got married," I said to Kekoa later that afternoon. Once Jeff dropped his bombshell all hell broke loose, so I'd called Luke to tell him the party was off and I'd try to stop by later that evening so we could discuss the case. While I hadn't learned a lot, Justin had said something that gave me an idea I wanted to explore further.

"Did your Mom flip out?"

Kekoa was still at work, so I'd stopped by the resort to fill her in on the latest gossip.

"Totally. Not only was Mom mad that Jeff married Candy but she was doubly mad that they'd eloped. There was one point when I seriously thought if she could have gotten her hands on Dad's gun she would have shot Candy."

"So what was your dad doing during all this?"

"At first he tried to play peacemaker between Jeff and Mom, but that only lasted for about five minutes and then he locked himself in his office with a bottle of whiskey. I know Jeff likes to stir things up—it's always been sort of his thing—but even I have to admit he was way out of line. Not only did he spring this huge thing on everyone, but he as much as said that if Mom wanted to be a part of his life or part of the lives of the children they planned to have, she was going to have to make amends with Candy for the way she'd treated her."

"Your mom treated Candy badly?"

"After Jeff and Candy broke up. Mom could see how bad Jeff was hurting, so she blamed her for the whole thing. She even went so far as to call her and say some really hurtful things. Jeff is the youngest boy and Mom babies him as much as she tries to baby me. I know her attitude toward Candy comes from a place of love, but things really got ugly. The only good thing to come out of it was that Jason was so busy trying to keep Mom from strangling Jeff that I managed to make my escape before he totally laid into me for sneaking into Cole's room."

"Do you think he knows I helped you?"

"No. I told Justin I used a key I'd found on the table next to where I'd found Cole's body. He seemed to buy it because they didn't actually find Cole's room key on his body. Which makes me wonder if the person who killed him took the key for some reason."

"You think the killer was in the room?"

"Maybe. It's a theory worth exploring."

I waited while Kekoa checked in a middle-aged couple who were visiting the resort for their anniversary. I wondered if I would ever find anyone I cared about enough to be married to for twenty-five years. From where I sat right now it seemed highly unlikely. Jason and Alana seemed happy enough, and I guess I could see them going the distance, but I had to agree with Mom that Jeff and Candy were heading for a train wreck.

It isn't that I don't like Candy. She's actually fun to hang out with, and she's only two years older than me, so we actually were good friends when she and Jeff were dating. The problem is that Candy has a short attention span. I know Jeff tells everyone their decision to split after high school was mutual, but Candy told me she had her sights on another guy long before the split actually happened. Looking back, I guess I should have told Jeff what I knew, but after they broke up I didn't see the point. The poor guy was devastated. The last thing I wanted to do was pour salt in the wound. I suppose now it was way too late to have that conversation.

"I get off at seven. Do you want to do something tonight?" Kekoa asked after she'd completed her task.

"Maybe. I need to stop by to talk to Luke. How about if I text you?"

"Luke?"

"It's about the case, nothing else. He knew Cole, and the background information he's been able to provide has been helpful. We both know I don't care for the guy, but I would be stupid not to accept his help."

Kekoa didn't say anything, but she grinned in such a way as to indicate that she could see my true intention in meeting with Luke, even if I wasn't willing to admit it myself.

"Invite Luke to the condo. We'll grab a pizza or something. I know I've been out of the loop on this whole Cole thing, but I want to help."

"Can you print me a history of his visits to the resort?"

Kekoa frowned. "I want to help, not get fired."

"Who will know?"

Kekoa sighed. "Okay. But don't tell anyone where you got the information if the subject should come up."

"Don't worry; I won't tell anyone you've helped me in anyway, even if I'm tortured. Print me a history for Patrick Anderson as well."

Kekoa did as I'd asked.

"I'll text you after I talk to Luke. Pizza sounds good, but if we go to the condo chances are we'll be joined by whoever else is around. Maybe we should just meet at Luke's. It's a lot more private and he has a great patio."

"That'd be cool. I've always wanted to check out his place. Is it okay if I ask Cam to come along?"

"As long as it's just Cam. If he had plans with Makena don't bring them. I think it's best at this point that we keep our investigation between us. Do you happen to know if Drake is working today? I wanted to ask him about a redhead I saw on the beach."

"Yeah, he's here. In fact, he's working command in the office today because Mitch is off. Did you hear that Mitch put in a request to personnel to formally promote Drake to his assistant?"

"What? Why Drake? Cam and I have been here longer, and we're both a lot more qualified."

Kekoa leaned in close. "You didn't hear this from me, but Kimo told me that he saw Mitch and Drake's aunt dancing and drinking into the wee hours of the morning on the night of the storm. I checked the records, and Mitch also used one of his comps for the hotel that night. If you ask me, things are heating up between them, and I'm sure Mitch is feeling the pressure to kiss up to Drake."

I rolled my eyes. Mitch was a nice guy and an okay boss, but he did tend to think with a part of his anatomy well south of his brain. If Drake was promoted to assistant director of the WSO team, I was going to have no choice but to look for another job. The guy was an idiot.

"Do you think personnel will actually promote him over Cam and me?"

"Decisions about hiring, firing, and promotions are handled by the personnel department. All Mitch can really do is put in a recommendation. It's been my experience that the recommendation of the current supervisor is taken into account quite a lot. I'd say there's a good chance the promotion will go through."

"Great, and I thought hearing that Jason found my phone was going to be the worst news I'd hear all day."

There were some days when you realized you should have just stayed in bed. I was afraid today was shaping up to be one of them.

Chapter 7

I'm not sure how he did it, but somehow within thirty minutes of arriving at Luke's, he had me calmed down, relaxed, and focused on the case. I explained that neither Anderson nor Devlin were on the island at the time of Cole's death and that both men had commented that without him, the funding for the project was in jeopardy, and that Sean had said the resort owner who had hosted his stay in Mexico was of the opinion that Cole was using the land to scam investors even though he knew the project was doomed to fail. "What if one or both of Cole's partners found out about the scam and decided to get rid of him before they could be linked to his illegal activity?"

Luke frowned. It appeared he was considering my theory but wasn't fully sold. "The Branson Cole I remember might not always have looked really closely at the source of the money provided by the investors he worked with, but I don't see him intentionally scamming anyone. His connections were his livelihood. It would take only one scam on his part to undo a lifetime of relationship building. Maybe

Cole was raising funds based on his belief that the project was legitimate when in actuality one or both of his partners were up to no good. Maybe he found out about it and the partner who was really behind the scam had him killed."

"I guess we can't know until we find the killer. The person who slipped the toxin into Cole's drink had to have been someone on the beach that day. I still suspect both the brunette who brought Cole the drink and the redhead I spoke to on the beach. One or both of them might be the key to figuring this whole thing out."

"Are you sure there *was* a brunette? The redhead told you the drink was delivered by a brunette, but you really only have her word for it. Maybe the redhead was the one who poisoned Cole and she just wanted to throw you off by mentioning someone else."

I had to admit that was a possibility I hadn't considered. I was pretty sure the redhead had lied about at least part of what she'd told me. For one thing, she'd said she'd been there all day yet no one remembered seeing her, including Drake. Drake was a lousy safety officer, but he was a huge horn dog. The redhead was a beautiful woman. If she'd been on the beach all day Drake would have noticed her.

And she'd been the closest to the body when I left the beach with Kekoa. It was completely possible she was the one who'd taken the glass. Although if she was the one to poison Cole, why point out the glass in the first place? In fact, why would she show up at the crime scene at all? If she was the guilty party, it seemed she would have been long gone by the time it was discovered Cole was dead.

I was trying to make up my mind about what to do next when my phone dinged, informing me I had a text. It was Kekoa.

"I told Kekoa I was coming over to discuss the murder with you and she wondered if she and Cam could join us. I've been speaking to both of them about my efforts, so they know what's going on."

"Certainly. I'd love to have them stay for dinner. I have some steaks I can barbecue. Tell them to bring suits if they want to swim."

I relayed the information to Kekoa while Luke went inside to defrost the meat. It was quiet and peaceful on Luke's patio. I could see why he loved spending time out here. The sound of the waterfall was relaxing and the cool breeze from the coast must make for very pleasant evenings. I wondered if Luke got lonely up here on his horse ranch all by himself. Of course he had Brody for company. I guess I could see why he kept him around.

I took out the lodging histories for Branson Cole and Patrick Anderson. I'm not sure what I was looking for, but I found it odd that they had never stayed at the resort at the same time. I wondered how they'd met. I seemed to remember Kimo saying Anderson had said it was Devlin who'd both approached Anderson and brought Cole to the table. Maybe the key to this whole thing was in figuring out exactly who Devlin was and what role he might play in the scam, if there even was a scam.

Jason had mentioned speaking to Devlin, which meant he most likely had a file on him. I was pondering the implications of trying to get another look at his computer when my phone rang. I looked at the caller ID. It was Alana.

"Hey, sis, what's up?" Although Alana and I weren't actually sisters, we'd taken to referring to each other in that manner after she'd married Jason.

"I'm just calling to give you a heads-up that Jason is on his way to your condo to confront you about the photos he found on your phone. Thanks to a very tense afternoon trying to keep your mom from strangling Candy, he isn't in a good mood, and at this point I wouldn't put it past him to arrest you for your own well-being."

"Luckily I'm not at home, nor do I plan to be at home anytime soon, but I appreciate the warning. Are you still at Mom's?"

"No, the kids and I are home now. Jason dropped us off before heading to your place. Can you believe the bombshell Jeff dropped? I'm not sure I've ever seen your mom that mad."

"It did seem like Jeff meant to announce his marriage to Candy in a way that would guarantee maximum carnage. Sometimes I don't get him. I know he thinks it's fun to stir things up, but in this case I'm afraid he might actually have damaged his relationship with Mom. They've always been really close. In fact, Jeff is probably—or maybe I should say *was* probably—the closest to Mom of all us kids."

"Maybe that was it. Maybe he wanted to put some distance in the relationship. Your mom does tend to coddle him. Probably even more than she coddles you."

"Yeah, I guess, but all he's done is cement the fact that Mom is never going to accept Candy into the family. If Jeff really wanted her to be welcomed, he should have slowed things way down and let Mom get used to the idea that she was back."

Sandy must have noticed the stress in my voice because he got up from his spot in the shade and wandered over to put his head in my lap. I lazily scratched him behind the ears.

"Did you leave before Mom threatened Jeff with her big frying pan?" Alana asked.

I couldn't help but laugh. Mom was only an inch taller than me and just as thin, whereas Jeff was a good six three and built like a Mack truck. "Yeah, I guess I did. I'm sorry I missed that. I would have stayed for the whole show, but Justin told me Jason found my phone, so I used the diversion to make my escape."

"Good thinking. Now is probably not the best time to try to explain yourself to Jason. He's really worked up and who knows if he's thinking clearly?"

"He's too overprotective."

Alana didn't answer right away. When she did there was a seriousness in her voice that hadn't been there before. "I called you because I don't think this is the best time for you and Jason to chat, but I *am* concerned about your actions. You could have gotten yourself killed. You aren't a cop and you don't have a gun. I don't think any of us believes what you did was justified. Jason might be hard on you at times, but it's because he loves you and doesn't want to see you get hurt."

"But he treats me like a baby."

"No, he treats you like a person who, at times, demonstrates a lack of common sense. He treats you like a person who, at times, only thinks of herself and not how her actions will affect others. It occurred to me after I found out about the photos that the reason you came by the other morning was most likely to snoop. Very uncool."

Great. Now I'd made Alana mad. That was the last thing I wanted to do.

"I'm sorry. I shouldn't have tried to pump you for information about the case." I decided not to mention that I'd hacked into Jason's computer. That would really make everyone mad. "I really just want Jason and everyone else to take me seriously. I've wanted to be a cop my whole life, but as long as my well-meaning family keeps using their connections to make certain I'll never get a shot I have no choice but to leave the islands or give up my dream. It's not fair."

"No, it's not fair," Alana agreed. "I've tried to talk to Jason about the subject, but he's just so dang protective of you. Still, he's not wrong about the fact that you're impulsive, and an impulsive cop is too often a dead cop."

I took a deep breath and let it out slowly. "Look, you make a good point. I promise not to play Spider-Man the next time Jason catches me in a compromising position."

"Spider-Man?"

It took quite a lot of quick talking to explain away the Spider-Man comment without actually telling Alana about my balcony escape. I was already in trouble with my older brother. If he found out exactly how I'd managed to avoid him, he'd lock me up and throw away the key for sure.

By the time I got off the phone with Alana, Luke had returned to the patio.

"Problems?" he asked.

"That was my sister-in-law warning me that my brother is on his way to my condo to read me the riot act about breaking into Cole's suite. I guess it's a good thing I'm not home. Hopefully by the time I do get there he'll have given up on the idea at least for today. This thing between Jeff and my mom has him all worked up and

Alana is afraid he's going to take out his frustrations on me."

"What about tomorrow?"

"I'm off work, so as long as I get up really early and head somewhere Jason won't think to look for me I should be safe."

"I have plenty of guest rooms if you and Sandy want to stay here."

Oh, boy, was that a bad idea. "Thanks; I just might. If I call Kekoa before she comes out I can have her bring me my toothbrush and a change of clothes." As I said it, I realized I was never going to hear the end of it from Cam, but a little teasing seemed like the better choice compared to being ripped a new one by Jason. "Thanks for the offer."

"Trust me, I feel your pain. I know how it is when a family member thinks they know what's better for you than you do."

"Sounds like something specific."

"My sister called yesterday to let me know that an old friend was coming to the island next month and she'd assured her I would be fine with her staying with me."

"So? That sounds nice."

"The friend is one of my sister's best friends and it seemed obvious that matchmaking was very much on my sister's mind."

"Ouch."

"Ouch is right. It's not that I have any ill feelings toward this woman. She's a nice person and I actually like her. It's just that I know her feelings for me are somewhat other than just being friends, and my sister has hopes the two of us will hook up once I decide it's time to settle down. In fact, she's actually said as much."

"What are you going to do?"

Luke shrugged. "I guess I'm going to have to let her stay here. My sister already made the offer and I hate to make a big deal out of it. I just hope I can protect my virtue," he teased. "The woman is a barracuda."

I laughed. "If it helps, I can pretend to be your girlfriend while she's here."

"I just might take *you* up on that."

I was kidding when I made the offer, but something told me that Luke was quite serious. How did I get myself into these things?

"I'm going to head over to the barn to check on the horses before Cam and Kekoa get here. Do you want to come?"

I found I actually did. I know what I've said about horses and I have absolutely not changed my mind, but I welcomed the chance to get another peek at Lucifer.

Chapter 8

Monday, March 14

The room was dark, but I could sense the first light of day beyond the drawn blinds. I turned slightly toward the window and groaned when I felt a weight next to me in the king-size bed where I'd slept off way too much of Luke's expensive wine. The temptation to go back to sleep was great. I was afraid that if I opened my eyes I would see Luke lying next to me, and that was something I was definitely not up for. I was calculating the odds of sliding out of the bed, out of the room, and out of Luke's life once and for all when I felt something wet on my cheek.

I slowly opened my eyes and smiled in relief when I saw Sandy staring back at me. A quick glance confirmed that we were the only two in the bed, which left me with such an abundance of relief that I actually felt the remnants of my hangover melting away.

I slid out of bed and pulled on the shorts and sweatshirt that were laying across the chair; I'd awakened in nothing but a bra and underwear. I remembered Cam and Kekoa leaving before Luke opened the fourth bottle of wine, and for the life of me, I couldn't remember undressing myself. I suppose it was possible I had but didn't remember due to my state of inebriation, but the truth was I was a slob when it came to undressing at night and tended to leave my clothes where they fell until the next morning. Chances were someone else had folded them neatly and left them on the chair.

My cheeks burned red when I realized Luke must have undressed me and put me to bed. I was beyond embarrassed, although my bra and panties were no skimpier than the bikinis I often wore, so it wasn't like I'd really been indecent. Still, to be so totally wasted that I couldn't even remember what had happened wasn't the impression I wanted to make on the very together and sophisticated man I'd shared a house with overnight.

There was a large pot of coffee waiting when I finally wandered into the kitchen. Next to the coffee was a bottle of aspirin and a note from Luke, saying he'd be back soon. I took two of the aspirin with a glass of water, poured a mug of coffee, added a dollop of milk, and headed out to the patio.

It was going to be a beautiful day. Although the sun had not yet risen over the horizon, the sky was clear and the air temperature pleasantly warm. I pulled up one of the lounge chairs, turning it to face the east to watch the sun rise, then settled in while Sandy ran around the area sniffing everything in sight. I hadn't seen any sign of Duke or Dallas, so I assumed Luke had taken them with him wherever he went.

"Well, who do we have here?" Brody teased. "Is it little Lani Pope doing the walk of shame?"

"I'm not walking and nothing happened." I placed my hand to my pounding head. At least I didn't think anything happened. I really couldn't be sure because I didn't remember much after Cam and Kekoa left.

Brody didn't say anything as he sat down next to me with his own cup of coffee.

"Too much wine," I felt compelled to explain.

Brody laughed. "Been there. That imported stuff Luke has really packs a punch. I'm not sure what the alcohol content is, but I'm guessing it's a lot higher than the boxed stuff you and I are used to."

"Do you happen to know where Luke might have gone?" I wondered.

Brody pointed to a bluff in the distance. It was higher than the piece of land the ranch was built on and must have afforded a fantastic view of the sea to the east.

"Keep an eye on that flat part at the top. I'm betting Luke and company will appear at any moment."

No sooner had Brody said as much than Luke, sitting high atop a horse, appeared as a silhouette in the distance with the rising sun just beyond him.

"How'd you know he'd gone to watch the sunrise?"

"He does almost every morning. At least on the hot days. He likes to exercise his horses before the main heat of the day sets in. Those two little dots you see next to Luke are Duke and Dallas."

The image of Luke sitting high atop a large, dark-colored horse as the sun set in the background brought chills to my spine in spite of the fact that it wasn't at all cold.

"Wow," I let slip.

Brody smiled. "Wow the sunrise or wow the man on the horse?"

"Both," I answered honestly.

Brody and I sat in silence as the sun rose into the sky. Once it was fully visible in the distance Luke turned and headed back.

"So how is it you happened to be here drinking Luke's wine in the first place?" Brody asked. "I thought you didn't like him."

"I don't. I mean didn't. It's confusing."

Brody grinned.

"It was all very innocent. Cam, Kekoa, and I were here to discuss the Branson Cole murder. If you remember, Luke knew Cole from Texas, and I thought he might have some insight."

"Are Cam and Kekoa sleeping it off as well?"

"No. They had to work so they left."

Brody didn't say anything, but I could tell what he was thinking.

"Nothing happened. I swear. I think I'm going in."

"Before you do, I have something I was going to track you down to show you today, but as long as you're here and we're talking about Cole's death…"

Brody pulled out his phone and began looking for something. Then he handed it to me. It showed a photo of the scene on the day I'd found Cole's body. I could clearly see both the glass on the table and the redhead I'd been talking to.

"Where'd you get this?"

"Trent."

Trent was a local who liked to surf the waves off the resort beach.

"I worked tower two yesterday and we got to chatting. He claimed to have photos of the dead guy we'd found. I asked to see them and he showed me these."

"These?"

"Thumb through."

I did and found a series of photos. Obviously Trent was more interested in getting a shot of the body than anything else. There were other people in the photos, but all you could really make out were body parts: a leg here, an arm there, the edge of someone's swim trunks. The first photo—the one where you could clearly see the redhead—had been taken at a distance, but the remainder of the photos were taken using the zoom. The one interesting thing I noticed was that between photo four and photo five the glass disappeared. Photo six clearly showed I was still speaking to the redhead, so it couldn't have been her who'd taken the glass.

The question was, who had?

"Do we know who any of these other spectators are?"

"Trent didn't remember. You were there; don't you remember?"

"No. The redheaded woman walked up and I spoke to her until Kekoa came over, at which point I turned my attention to her."

I looked at the photos more carefully. There was a man with blue swim trunks standing near the victim's head. I knew it was a man only because the legs that was featured in the photo were clearly those of a man. There was also a woman in a red bikini standing somewhat farther back but still close enough for the camera to pick up her torso from the waist down. None of the partial knees, elbows, or shoulders were identifiable at all. I tried to remember whether I'd noticed the man in the blue trunks or the woman in the red bikini at the time, but I was coming up blank.

"Will you send me a copy of all these photos?"

"I already did. I guess you haven't checked your phone since last night."

"No," I admitted, "I haven't. Do you recognize any of these body parts?"

Brody shook his head. "There isn't enough of any one person to be able to identify them. The body was low to the ground. Trent must have been standing on something because it appears he was aiming his camera down toward Cole. With the exception of that first photo, no one is visible from the waist up."

The photos told me the redheaded woman hadn't taken the glass, and that was important. I just wasn't sure how I was going to figure out which knee, elbow, or leg belonged to the person who had.

When Luke returned from his ride he made a fantastic breakfast for all three of us. I have to say that Luke's cooking went a long way toward curing my headache. I asked Brody to talk to Trent again if he saw him at the resort today. Maybe Trent recognized someone in the crowd. He'd had the advantage of seeing the whole person and not just the knee or elbow he'd photographed. Maybe he remembered seeing someone he knew. At the very least I was willing to bet he'd noticed the girl in the red bathing suit. There was no way Trent would see that body through the lens of his camera and not stop to take a closer look.

"So what sort of plans do you have for today?" Luke asked after Brody finished his meal and left to get ready for work.

"Senior bingo."

"Come again?"

I explained about providing Elva with a ride to lunch with her friends and senior bingo on Mondays. "You can come along if you want. I'm sure the seniors won't mind."

Luke shrugged. "I don't have any specific plans. It might be fun. When I was a kid I used to go to senior bingo with my grandmother. It was a blast."

"Perfect. I usually pick Elva up at eleven."

"We'll take my car. You can just leave Sandy here with the boys. He really seems to enjoy the company."

"Yeah, he does seem to like it here. If I had a bigger place, I'd get a second dog to keep him company when I'm at work."

"Sandy is welcome to come to visit any time. Even when you're working."

"Thanks; I might take you up on that sometime."

Elva was thrilled to be escorted to lunch and bingo by a handsome cowboy who lathered on the southern charm to make sure she felt as if she were the most beautiful and fascinating woman in the world. The coffee shop at which the Monday afternoon bingo group always met was really just a run-down diner that offered simple food in abundant quantities at reasonable prices. Because it was well off the beaten path, more often than not it was locals who patronized the clean but shabby eatery.

"Woo wee. Where did you women get this fine piece of eye candy?" asked Wilma Goodwin, the fifty-four-year-old owner of the coffee shop. Wilma was as loud and outspoken as she was ample, but she'd been a fixture in the area for so long that most people considered her presence as comforting as the food she whipped up every day.

"He's a friend of Lani's," Elva answered.

Wilma looked directly at me and winked. "You go girl. Always wanted to sleep with a cowboy."

"We're just friends."

"Yeah, I'll bet you are." Wilma chuckled. "What can I get you, sweetheart?"

"I'll have the grilled cheese and fries with a side of ranch," I ordered.

"And how about you, babycakes?" Wilma asked Luke.

"I'll have the same."

"I'm single, ya know. In case you were wondering."

Luke simply smiled.

Wilma gave Luke a glance that was certain to convey her interest in a hookup of the physical kind before turning her attention toward Elva, who ordered a cheeseburger and onion rings.

I know it may seem gross that a fifty-four-year-old woman would be so blatantly coming on to a thirty-two-year-old man, but Wilma comes on to everyone. I can't really explain it, but Wilma's flirty outer core seemed to work for her, and more often than not her intended victims were more amused than offended.

Once everyone at the table had ordered Elva began the introductions. "Luke, I'd like you to meet Susan, Connie, Beth, Janice, Lucy, and Diane."

All six of the women smiled at Luke as they individually greeted and welcomed him to the group. When I first began accompanying Elva on Mondays I was expecting to be bored by the conversation in which seven senior women were likely to engage, but I found out rather quickly that they were both intelligent and hysterically opinionated.

"So, Luke, what do you do for a living?" Susan Oberman, the youngest member of the Monday afternoon group at sixty, asked.

"At the moment I'm focusing my energy on remodeling my home and establishing my stable."

"So you have a lot of time on your hands?"

"I wouldn't say a lot, but, yeah, I guess I have more than most. Why?"

"I'm the chairperson for the upcoming coastal cleanup day and we sure could use all the help we can get. Especially a man with your particular build who can help with the larger items. Interested?"

"Absolutely. When is it?"

"A week from Saturday."

"Okay, I'll try to make it."

Susan was a happily married woman who had delivered and raised four children, but when Luke agreed to help with her project she grinned in a way that reminded me of a cat who'd managed to capture the tastiest mouse in town.

"I could use some help with my rain gutters," Lucy Sanchez hastily added. "Maybe sometime this week? I can make us lunch. With pie for dessert. Apple. I'm pretty sure I read somewhere that you cowboys like apple pie, being that it's so American and all."

Luke shot Lucy a smile as well. "I'd be happy to stop by."

I could see the fine women of the Monday afternoon bingo group were going to monopolize all Luke's time if I didn't intervene. Apparently *no* or *I'm busy* were not in the man's repertoire of possible responses.

"So how was your date last weekend?" I asked Janice Furlong. Janice was the oldest member of the group at seventy-four. For some reason, after almost forty years of widowhood, she'd decided she wanted to get married again and had signed up for an online dating service catering to men and women sixty years of age or older.

"It was a bust. All the men on that site are old. I'm looking for someone younger. Someone with more energy. Someone like Luke."

"Luke is younger than your youngest son," I reminded Janice. "Other than the fact that the man you chose was age appropriate, what didn't you like about him?"

"He likes to watch the *CBS Evening News* and I'm an ABC sort of gal. It'd never work out. Besides, he mentioned he takes medication for his heart. I'm not looking to bury another man any time soon. Is your brother John still single? I always did have a thing for him."

"John is single, but he's thirty-eight. Did you ever call to find out about the yoga class the senior center sponsors? I'm sure a lot of the men in that class are both single and healthy."

"Looking to party, not exercise. I did meet a nice man in a bar last week. He's probably in his early sixties, which is a little old for me, but the guy was a nice dresser and seemed to have a lot of money, so I agreed to have a drink with him."

"And how do you know he has a lot of money?"

"He's part of that investment group that plans to build that new resort down the beach from where you work."

That got my attention. "Did he mention his name?"

"Of course he mentioned his name. We had a drink together."

"Are you willing to share it?"

"Frank Browning."

"And did he say why he was in town?"

"To meet with the man who died. Branson Cole. I wonder if he ever did get a chance to speak with him. Such a shame to come all that way for nothing."

Frank Browning. The name didn't sound familiar, but if he was in town to meet with Cole and Cole ended up dead, you could bet I was going to find out everything I could about him.

Kekoa called me just as bingo was letting out to inform me that Patrick Anderson had checked into the resort and that he was in the bar meeting with a man with dark hair. I asked Kekoa to try to find out who the man was. I intended to drop in for a drink of my own, but in the event that the man left before I arrived I wanted Kekoa to get as much information as she could.

"Where to?" Luke asked after he spoke to Diane Francis about helping her repaint her guest bedroom. Hadn't these women heard of handymen?

"Dolphin Bay. After we take Elva home, that is. Kekoa called while you were talking to Diane and informed me that Patrick Anderson is in the bar meeting with another man. Suddenly I think a drink sounds like a very good idea."

"And you aren't worried about Jason showing up as well?"

"I have no idea whether Jason even knows Anderson is in town, but the meeting could provide an important lead, so I think I want to risk it."

Luke shrugged and helped me climb into the backseat of his truck before

165

helping Elva into the passenger seat in the front. After everyone was buckled up he headed toward the condo.

"Don't forget about the yarn store," Elva reminded me.

Oh, yeah. I had completely forgotten about the yarn store. I still hadn't met Mary and Malia, but I knew how important the afghan Elva was crocheting for Malia was to Elva, so I directed Luke to take a side trip in the opposite direction. Trying to get a peek at the man Anderson was meeting could be important to my investigation into Cole's death, but my heart went out to Elva. I couldn't imagine losing a child or, even worse, dealing with the grief of that loss while your marriage imploded at the same time. I'd always been curious as to the facts surrounding the tragedy that had defined the remainder of Elva's life, but she seemed to have dealt with things in her own way and I never wanted to push her to speak about that terrible time from her past.

"Emily loved blue," Elva said as she sorted through the blue yarn, looking for the perfect shade. "She used to say, 'Mama, I want a blue one just like the sky and just like the sea.'"

"Blue is one of the best colors," I agreed.

"I remember one year Emily wanted me to make her a blue and white dress for the Christmas concert at school. I tried to explain that the traditional colors for Christmas were red and green, and that the teacher had requested that all the students in the choir wear either red or green, but she said that deep blue was the color of the dark sky on the night Jesus was born and white was the color of the bright star in the sky. What better colors, she argued, to represent the most sacred of all nights?"

"She really had a good point."

A look of sadness came over Elva's face. "Yeah, she really did. I made her that blue and white dress and she wore it proudly in a sea of red and green." Elva looked down at the yarn in her hand. "I think this one will work best for the blanket. It's a happy blue that I hope will brighten Malia's life."

After we dropped Elva off at her condo, Luke and I headed toward the resort. I really had no idea if Anderson and his guest would still be in the bar after all this time, but I wouldn't have missed Elva's story about her daughter for anything. I guess I was lucky. So far I'd never lost anyone close to me other than senior members of my family, who'd lived good lives and passed due to complications brought about by old age.

When we arrived at the bar I saw Anderson sitting at a table in the corner with a man with dark hair whose back was to us. I didn't want to look conspicuous, so Luke and I ordered drinks, then settled in at a table I hoped was close enough for us to overhear at least part of their conversation.

The men seemed to be talking about golf. I wasn't sure how a conversation about golf was going to help me with my investigation, but I listened in anyway. The man who sat across from Anderson seemed to know a lot about the planning that went into designing a golf course, and it occurred to me that perhaps he was speaking to him about designing one for the new resort. Of course if the resort was really just a front for a scam I didn't know why you'd go to all the effort of interviewing architects and contractors for the various aspects of the project.

"Do you think they're talking about a golf course for the new resort?" I whispered to Luke.

He shrugged. "Maybe. It makes sense the resort would have a golf course and that the design would be included in the master plan. Anderson is the man we understand is in charge of planning the enterprise, so it makes sense that he'd be meeting with a potential architect."

"Are we thinking that the intel we received suggesting the resort is a front for a scam is false, or that Anderson simply isn't aware of that fact?"

Luke took a sip of his drink and leaned in close. I'm sure to anyone who might be watching us it looked like we were having an intimate conversation. "Like I said before, I would be very surprised to find out Branson was scamming his contacts. If the whole thing is a scam I'm betting he, and perhaps Anderson too, had no idea what was really going on."

"Something got Cole killed," I pointed out.

Luke took a deep breath. "Yeah, something did."

He and I continued to listen as the men discussed golf and the pros and cons of a high verses a low par course. I wasn't a player, so I didn't understand any of it, but I was enjoying spending time with Luke, and I could see he was actually interested in the conversation. After about twenty minutes, both men stood up, shook hands, and the dark-haired one walked away.

I watched as Anderson took out his phone and made a call.

"He seems to be on board," Anderson said.

I continued to watch as he played with the cherry stem from his drink while he listened to whoever was on the other end of the line. I couldn't be certain Anderson was guilty of either murder or scamming the investors who'd bought into his project, but his body language was relaxed and his demeanor didn't seem to indicate that he was worried about anyone overhearing his conversation.

"We can work out the details later. For now, I'm going to go ahead with the plan we outlined before Cole died. I spoke to Elton, and he seemed open to the idea I presented. Now that we have the permits and a green light to break ground I'm betting we'll have investors lining up."

Anderson almost looked bored as he listened to the response on the other end of the line. I wondered who Elton was and how he figured into everything that was going on. Of course the idea Elton was open to might not have anything to do with the resort.

"Yes, I agree that was unfortunate, but I'm not sure what we can do about it at this point." A flash of irritation crossed

Anderson's face. At least I thought it was irritation. I didn't know him well enough to really read his face, but his frown, combined with an aura of impatience, suggested irritation to me. "Tell Devlin I'll have the completed blueprints by the end of the month. Did you ever get back to Colton?"

Anderson took a sip of his drink while he listened. "And…?" Anderson smiled. "That's good. That's very, very good."

He put a hand up in the air to indicate to the bartender that he wanted another drink. It seemed Anderson didn't have an issue with his heart the way Cole had, judging by the way he seemed to be putting away the liquor. There was a stack of empties on his table.

"I need to get going," Anderson began to wrap things up. "Did you ever speak to that detective who came snooping around?" He frowned. "Yeah. Okay. Let me know how it goes."

With that, Anderson hung up. He downed the drink the bartender had just delivered, threw a stack of money on the table, got up, and walked out of the bar.

"What do you make of all that?" I asked Luke.

"It sounds like the project is on track, which runs counter to what we've heard, but it does seem like something's up. I wonder who he was speaking to."

"At first I thought maybe it was Devlin, but then he referred to him in a third-person way. He also mentioned Elton and Colton. They aren't unique names, but they aren't frequently used either. Does either ring a bell?"

"Maybe. I know a man named Elton who could very well have been approached to invest in the project if my dad was approached. I'd need to make some phone calls to know for sure. Do you want to stick around here or head back to the ranch?"

"I want to head over to the beach to see if I can find Trent. He's almost always surfing at this time of day and I'm hoping he'll remember something more about the people he shot with his camera. Then let's head back to your place. It's unlikely my brother will track me down there."

"You're going to have to face him at some point."

"Yeah, I know. But the longer I can avoid an encounter the more time he'll have to cool down. Besides, I think we're close to figuring this out."

"We are?" There was a look of doubt on Luke's face.

"We are," I said with more conviction than I actually felt.

Luckily, Trent, as expected, was surfing. I managed to catch his eye and waved him over, thereby avoiding having to actually get into the water. Luke said he was going to head over to the tower to talk to Cam, who was the WSO on duty that day. I told him I'd look for him there when I'd finished my conversation.

"Hey, Lani. What's up?" Trent greeted me as he waded out of the water. "I thought you were off today."

"I am. I stopped by to ask you about the photos you took of Branson Cole the day he died. Brody showed them to me this morning, and I hoped maybe you remembered some additional details about the people standing around the body."

"Sorry; I was really just focused on the body once I realized the old guy was dead."

"What about the girl in the red bikini?"

Trent smiled. "Now her I remember. Tall, blond, killer bod?"

Sounded familiar. I did think I remembered seeing her. "She had on those big earrings and her hair was pulled up on top of her head?"

"I wasn't looking at her hair, but that sounds right."

The more I thought about it the more certain I was that I remembered the woman. She had a tattoo just below her collarbone. I couldn't remember what it was, but the longer I concentrated on the woman the more I remembered.

"Do you have other photos you didn't show Brody?"

"Not of that particular moment, but I do have another photo of the lady in the red bikini. I'd seen her earlier in the day. She was watching the old guy who died while he was talking to the hot brunette. She had an interesting look on her face, so I snapped a photo of her."

"You saw Cole talking to a brunette?"

"Yeah. The one who brought him the drink."

"Did you get a photo of her?"

"No. Just the lady in the red bikini."

"Do you still have that other photo of the woman in the red bikini?"

"Yeah, it's on my phone. I took a bunch of photos that day for a photography class I'm taking online."

"You can study photography online?"

"We take photos and then choose three to share each week. I'm actually one of the best students in the class. My instructor said I have a real eye for framing the perfect shot."

I thought about all the partial body parts Trent had captured while taking photos of Cole. They didn't seem particularly artful to me. "Does this class cost money?"

"A bunch. But it's worth it."

Sounded like a scam to me, but I didn't say so. Trent seemed happy with his hobby and I supposed that was what really mattered.

"Can I see the photo of the lady in the red bikini?"

"Sure. It's one of my best. My phone is in my backpack, which I left in the tower. I'll get it."

"I'll come with you. Luke is waiting for me there anyway."

I had to admit Trent had managed to catch the expression of the woman perfectly. She looked both intent and contemplative. If I had to guess I'd say she had something other than sunbathing or surfing on her mind.

Chapter 9

It turned out the Elton Luke knew was the same one Patrick Anderson had referred to on the phone. Like Luke's dad, Elton had been approached early on by Cole and, also like Luke's dad, he'd turned him down when his research turned up some disturbing facts.

"So what changed his mind?" I wondered.

"I guess CAD Development somehow managed to address all the environmental and zoning issues presented to them and they were awarded permits to break ground this summer. Elton said once he confirmed the permits were legit he decided to jump onto what he was assuring me will end up being a money train. He even encouraged me to invest."

"Are you going to?"

"No. I have other plans for my money."

I sighed as I sat back in my chair.

"Is there a problem?" Luke asked.

"Not really. It's just that pretty much my entire theory regarding who might have killed Cole was based on dirty goings-on with CAD Development. If everything is on the up-and-up I really have no idea what the motive might have been for killing him."

"The motive might not have had anything to do with the project."

"I'm beginning to realize that. The thing is, I don't have any other ideas."

"What about the girlfriend my dad mentioned?"

I'd forgotten about that. "What was her name again?"

"Dad said Helena. He didn't have a last name."

I sat forward in my chair. Maybe Luke was on to something. "If Cole was seeing someone maybe we can ask around and find out who she is. We know he was staying at a motel in Honolulu the first three nights he was on the island and that he wasn't registered as staying anywhere else until he checked in at Dolphin Bay. Sean said Cole planned to stay with a woman, so I'm going to go out on a limb and guess the woman is this Helena."

"Makes sense, but how can we use that to track this Helena down?"

"I say ask around. What we need," I realized, "is the name of the hotel where Cole stayed when he first arrived on the island."

"Maybe there's a clue in the photos you took."

Luke logged onto his computer and we pulled up the file I'd e-mailed myself. At first I didn't see anything that would point us in a direction, but then I realized the note that had directed us to the bar had a pen laying across the bottom of it with the name of a motel near the airport.

"He might have picked this up on another trip, but I'm betting the Bayside Motor Lodge is where he stayed his first three nights."

"Isn't that place kind of a dive?" Luke asked.

"Yeah, it really is. I can't come up with a single reason why someone who can afford the tower suite at Dolphin Bay would stay there, but it's worth a road trip to check it out."

Luke shrugged. "I'm in. Let me grab my truck keys."

The road south was a beautiful one, but both Luke and I had driven it so many times that we used the time to get to know each other just a little bit better. I told him about my life growing up on the island and he told me about his growing up on a ranch in Texas. I'd never been to Texas and couldn't imagine a place with so much open space. Living on an island you get used to the compactness of everything. There wasn't anywhere you could go that would pose much of a commute, but the great state of Texas was so vast you could fit over 400 Oahus in it. The whole thing was mind-boggling.

"Favorite animal growing up?" Luke asked as part of our twenty-questions-to-getting-to-know-someone game.

"I didn't have any animals as a kid. I wanted one very badly, but Mom insisted that she had six children to feed and clean up after and wasn't going to spend one minute looking after a dog or cat. Sandy is actually the first pet I've ever had."

"That's so sad."

I shrugged. "It wasn't so bad. How about you? Who was your favorite pet as a kid?"

"My dog Rusty. He was a border collie my dad bought to help with the herding, but he broke his leg when he was young, so Dad let me make him a pet. I really loved that dog. I was devastated when he died. So much so that I promised to name my first child after him."

"What if you have a girl?"

"I think Rusty works equally well for a boy or a girl."

I laughed. "You know, I really expected you to say that your favorite animal was a horse."

"I learned to ride almost before I could walk and I had a lot of great horses through the years, but a horse can't sleep in your room or share your secrets the way a dog can. We had a lot of dogs on the ranch, but they were working animals and were really considered by everyone to belong to my dad. But Rusty was mine. I was the one he was most loyal to, unlike the others, who were well trained and obeyed anyone in the family but listened to my dad above all others."

Suddenly I found I missed Sandy. I usually spent a lot more time with him on my days off. Of course it looked as if he was having a blast with Duke and Dallas.

"Favorite childhood vacation?" Luke asked.

"I went to California with Kekoa's family when I was nine. We had the best time. We went to Disneyland and a real baseball game. My favorite part of the whole trip was Hollywood. I kept expecting to see someone famous, but I never did. Still, it was fun to look. How about you? What was your favorite vacation?"

"Our family didn't take a lot of vacations. It's hard to get away when there are so many animals to take care of. But there was this one trip to Kentucky I'll always remember. I was twelve and my dad decided it was time I went to my first horse breeders' auction. I'm not talking about the auctions they have at the fair; I'm talking about a high-dollar auction for prize breeding stock. I remember being so excited to finally have some one-on-one time with my dad. He was a busy man and didn't really spend all that much time with my sisters and me. I guess he figured my older brothers actually provided him with some help, while we were more of a responsibility."

"How was it?"

"We never got there. There was a big storm and our plane was diverted to Denver."

"You were traveling from Texas to Kentucky and you ended up in Denver? How did that happen?"

"That's exactly what my father asked. At first Dad was upset that he was missing the auction and not all that much fun to be around, but then he finally accepted that he wasn't going to make it and began to relax. After that we had a wonderful time, talking and really getting to know each other."

"That's nice."

"Yeah. It was the best time we ever had as a father and son. My turn; what was your most embarrassing moment?"

"No way I'm answering that one. What's your favorite movie?"

We continued with the game until we pulled up in front of the motor lodge.

"Now what?"

"I guess we start with whoever is working the desk and see what we can find out," I answered.

"And you think that person is just going to tell us what they know?"

"Got any cash?"

"Yeah. I've got some."

"They'll tell us. Let me do the talking."

It turned out the desk clerk did remember Cole, and he also remembered that a woman showed up asking for him on the morning he checked out. The clerk didn't know the woman's name but confirmed that she was the same one in the photo we had. The question was, was this Helena, or were we looking for two different women?

"So what now?" Luke asked after we'd returned to the truck.

"I should probably head home. I have to work tomorrow and I never did do my laundry."

"Do you want to grab some dinner on the way back? I know a great steak house. My treat."

I looked down at my casual clothes. "I'm not really dressed for a steak house."

"You're dressed fine for this one. Trust me; you'll love it."

Luke was right. I did love it. The steak house was not only charmingly Texan in décor but it featured local Kobe beef that was cooked to perfection.

"This might possibly be the best thing I've ever had in my mouth," I gushed as a country band played in the background. "What's in that sauce?"

"I don't claim to know all the ingredients, but it really does bring out the taste of the beef. How are your potatoes?"

"Delicious. How'd you find this place? I've never even heard of it."

"It's only been here for a year, so it isn't all that popular yet. One of the guys in the band likes to hang out at the beach where I surf sometimes, and when he found out I was from Texas he told me about it. It turns out the man who owns it is a transplant from Texas, just like me. We hit if off right away."

"Well, with the exception of the fact that the servers are all wearing chaps over their jeans and holsters on their hips, it's a great place. I'll need to come back sometime."

I watched as several of the patrons wandered onto the dance floor. I was having the best time with Luke. I know I'm being repetitive, but if you had told me even a day ago that I would be dining with Luke in a cowboy steak house and having the time of my life I would have thought you were crazy.

"I've been thinking about the woman from the bar." I decided to get my head out of the clouds and back in the game. "If the woman Cole met after he'd been here just a few days was the same one who met the man in the bar, as we suspect, maybe she's the one who killed him."

"That had occurred to me as well. He arrived on the island, where he holed up in a dive for three days. The woman we're referring to as the woman in the bar showed up at the motel and they left. He went off the radar until he checked into the Dolphin Bay Resort. Three days later a toxin was added to his drink and, if the redhead you spoke to is to be believed, the drink was brought to him by a woman with dark hair."

"It really does look like this woman could be the killer. She knew about the meeting at the Jungle. The only thing I'm not sure about is how to prove it."

"Maybe it's time to loop in your brother. I'm sure he has resources for finding out who the woman in the photo is, and he certainly has the authority to question Anderson in a more formal way than we would be able to."

I hated to admit it, but Luke was right. It was time to talk to Jason. "I'll stop by on my way to work tomorrow. Maybe I can distract him with the information we've been able to dig up and he won't yell at me for too long. If nothing else, if I stop by on my way to work I have a built-in escape if I need it."

"Sounds like you've thought this through."

"I have, but only in the past few minutes while we were sitting here. We should probably go. It looks like I'm going to have a long day tomorrow."

Chapter 10

Tuesday, March 15

Here's the thing about brothers. Or at least my brothers. I love them and I know they'd die for me, but there are times, such as today, when they can be a total pain in the ass. I'd called Jason that morning and told him I was ready to talk. I asked if he could stop by my condo before I had to leave for work and he told me it would be better under the circumstances if I stopped by the station. The station? Really? What was he planning to do, arrest me?

I'd like to think the answer to that was no, but Alana had said he was pretty mad, and I had spent the past day and a half avoiding him. I figured if push came to shove I'd simply swear my phone had been stolen and the incriminating photos he'd found had actually been taken by someone other than myself. Of course I'd already admitted to both Justin and Alana that I'd taken the photos, but I supposed I'd deal with that if I had to.

I'll admit I was starting to sweat just a bit in spite of the fact that I'd done my homework and had information to trade to Jason in exchange for a decrease in the amount of yelling I was sure he planned to do. For one thing, Luke had helped me track down Janice's date, Frank Browning. It seemed that, like Elton, Frank had been approached by Cole about investing in the project, and also like Elton, he'd initially declined. He'd been in town this past week to speak to Cole for a second time after discovering that somehow CAD Development had managed to do the impossible and clear up all the roadblocks to the project to gain the permits they so desperately needed.

Not only had he confirmed what Elton had told us but he'd provided an interesting piece of information when Luke asked if he'd met with one of the other men since Cole's death. He reported that yes, the meeting had taken place, with the lead partner in the project, Helena Devlin.

Wow! I know, right? Helena and Devlin were one and the same. I'm really not sure if that makes me suspect her of killing Cole more or less. Luke forwarded the photo I took of the woman in the bar and Frank confirmed that the woman we saw was indeed Helena Devlin.

So, you ask, what am I thinking? Honestly, I have no idea.

I spent the entire drive to the precinct trying to decide how all these random pieces of information fit together.

Based on the information I'd gathered, the project had originated with Devlin, who we now knew was also Helena, the woman Cole had been bragging about dating. If that was correct, Helena had approached Anderson first about the project, so I could assume she knew him well enough to be aware he planned resorts for a living and might be interested in planning one of his own on the island. Devlin and Anderson knew they'd need seed money to buy the land, draw up the plans, and go through the permit process, so they'd brought Cole on board.

The woman Luke and I had seen in the bar was very beautiful and at least twenty years younger than Cole, so I wasn't sure where the romance came in unless Cole wasn't initially on board with the project and Helena needed to somehow convince him to use his connections to help them raise the money they needed.

Whatever the basis for their relationship, I knew Cole had come to the island for the last time a few weeks ago. He'd stayed in a dive motel for three days until Helena came looking for him. They left together and were off the radar for close to two weeks before Cole suddenly reappeared and rented the most expensive room at the very exclusive Dolphin Bay Resort. Three days later he was dead.

I suspected the toxin that killed Cole had been delivered in a drink, although apparently I was the only one who remembered seeing the glass. Of course now I had Brody's photos to back up my assertion, which should make Jason take me seriously on at least this one issue. During the time I was speaking to the redhead, who seemed to have disappeared, someone took the glass. The redhead had said the drink was delivered by a tall brunette, so I was going to assume it was Cole's girlfriend, Helena Devlin, who brought him that drink. That would explain why he stopped to speak to her and why it appeared she was flirting with him. Sort of. There was still the fact that he was old and plump while she was young and beautiful, but for now I was going to assume she still needed his financial connections.

The question remained, did Devlin kill Cole, and if so why? I supposed it was possible the toxin had been delivered in some other manner and the drink had nothing to do with it. Without the glass there was really no conclusive way to prove it one way or another. I did know that Devlin had met the man of Japanese descent in the bar the following day, but maybe she was already going to attend the meeting with Cole and her presence had nothing to do with his death. She'd handed him a thumb drive, but it could have contained anything. Maybe he was going to apply to be the resort's sushi chef and she was giving him the information he'd need. Okay, I don't really believe this, but the fact that she gave something to the man didn't prove she killed Cole.

When I began my drive I'd felt like I'd figured out a lot, but the more I thought about it the more I realized I really hadn't figured out anything. Or at least not anything Jason probably didn't already know. When I was listening in on his conversation with my dad, Jason had said he'd spoken to both Anderson and Devlin, so he already knew Devlin was a beautiful woman and not a man.

Suddenly I began to wonder if I really did have anything to offer to Jason in exchange for my neck out of a noose. I'd been running around for days chasing clues that suddenly seemed less like clues and more like insignificant pieces of information. I don't know why I thought I could solve Cole's death before the HPD. Maybe everyone was right and I wasn't cut out to be a cop.

I was feeling quite humbled and was prepared to go into the precinct, apologize to Jason, and head off to work with my tail between my legs when I noticed a woman who looked an awful lot like Helena Devlin coming out of the bank and getting into a white sedan that was waiting for her. Suddenly throwing in the towel was the last thing on my mind. I executed a quick U-turn and followed her.

I had no idea where this was going, and it did occur to me it might be a wild-goose chase that was going to make me late for both my meeting with Jason and work, but my gut told me that following the woman I'd suspected all along—okay, maybe not all along, but for a while now—was the only chance I had of saving face and solving this case.

Devlin seemed to be traveling back toward the north shore. It occurred to me that it might be a good idea to tell someone where I was going, so I dialed Luke's cell and left a message when he didn't pick up.

"Hey, Luke, it's Lani. I'm following a car in which Helena Devlin is traveling. We're heading in the general direction of your ranch, although we could turn off at any time. I assume you aren't meeting with the woman. If you are, this is going to be embarrassing. If not, I just wanted to fill you in on what I'm doing. Oh, wait, the car is turning onto a side road. I'll call you back."

I slowed down and hung back after the sedan turned onto what looked to be a private road. If I continued to follow in my car it was going to be obvious, so I pulled off the road and parked in some dense shrubbery. Then I headed down the road on foot. Chances were the white sedan's destination wasn't all that far away. I wasn't sure where we were exactly, but I was pretty sure the bluff to my right was the same one where Luke watched the sunrise; I was just on the other side.

By the time I'd traveled about a half mile I could see a building in the distance. It was a small house that had been built into the dense shrubbery, making it almost invisible. I got as close as I dared without risking someone seeing me. Of course I had no idea what I was going to do at this point. I couldn't get close enough to the house to look through the windows, so I really had no way of knowing what was going on inside. Maybe nothing. Holing up in an out-of-the-way house was certainly no crime.

I decided to call Luke again to see if he'd pick up this time. Maybe he would have an idea that hadn't occurred to me.

"It's Lani again," I began when Luke's voice mail picked up again. "I'm outside a house that I think is just over the bluff from your place. I was following…"

A hand was placed over my mouth from behind. Damn. How had someone snuck up on me without my knowing? I was really off my game.

"What are you doing here?" the voice behind me asked.

I pointed to the hand over my mouth to indicate that I couldn't answer, which might have been just as well because I really didn't *have* an answer.

"You're that lifeguard who found the body."

I nodded my head in the affirmative.

"I'm going to remove my hand from your mouth, but you aren't to make a sound."

I could feel a gun in my back, so it was a safe bet I'd comply.

A woman took her hand from my mouth and demanded that I turn around slowly. I did as she asked and was surprised to see not Helena Devlin but the woman from the beach who had been wearing a red bikini on the day Cole had died.

"Now I'm going to ask you again, what are you doing here?"

"I was hiking and got lost."

"Nice try. What are you really doing here?"

"Following Helena Devlin." I figured there was no reason to lie. The woman obviously knew what I was doing there.

"Why are you following Helena Devlin?"

"Because I thought maybe—" My answer was interrupted by a gunshot. I watched in horror as the chest of the woman I'd been speaking to turned red. I didn't stop to think about what I should do, I just reacted and took off running. I ran as hard and fast as I could, although even I knew I couldn't outrun a bullet. I could hear voices behind me, but still I ran, even though my legs were bleeding from the scratches of the dense shrubbery and my lungs felt like they were on fire from lack of oxygen. Luke's ranch was just over the bluff, if only I could keep going.

Just when I felt like I was going to pass out for sure I felt myself being scooped into the air. As the last of my breath was pushed from my lungs by the death grip around my chest, my feet flew helplessly through the air. I felt like I'd been scooped up by a giant eagle, like you see in sci-fi movies. There was no other explanation. I must be close to death because I was obviously hallucinating. I closed my eyes and let the dizziness overtake me.

"Are you okay?" a voice said in my ear.

I opened my eyes. "Luke?"

"Are you hurt?"

It took me a minute to realize I wasn't actually flying but riding. "Did you seriously just ride up on a white stallion and save me?"

Luke slowed the horse and smiled. "I guess I did."

I looked at the horse beneath me and the man who held me in his arms. Kailani Pope was no princess and she was no damsel in distress. I was afraid things with Luke were over before they'd begun because there was no coming back from this.

Chapter 11

Friday, March 18

"To Lani, who didn't solve the crime but did manage to snag the prince." Cam held up his glass in a toast.

"Bite me."

"Come on, Lani. You have to admit the whole thing was romantic," Kekoa encouraged. "I can't believe you still won't talk to Luke."

"If I'm ever going to be taken seriously as a prospective cop I can't have some knight in freakin' armor showing up to rescue me every time I get into a tiny bit of trouble."

"I know Sean and I just arrived home," Kevin commented, "but it sounds like you were in more than just a little trouble."

"I had it handled."

"Really?" Sean laughed. "What exactly were you going to do?"

"I don't know. I didn't have a chance to think things through."

"The Interpol agent you were talking to had just been shot. You were most likely next. Sure you ran, but even you have to admit you were running out of steam. If you ask me, Luke saved your life and you should be thanking him, not punishing him for bruising your huge ego."

Deep down I knew Sean had a point, but my ego *was* bruised, and blaming Luke was the only way I could see to save face. Okay, I know that doesn't make sense. Give me a break. It's been a tough week.

"Did Jason get the case wrapped up?" Carina asked.

"He did. I guess the agent—whose name is Mallari Baldini, by the way—had been investigating Helena Devlin all along. It seems I was right in my assertion that there was some funny business going on with the investments. Cole and Anderson were both totally innocent and honestly believed they were going to build a resort. Devlin was making just enough progress to keep everyone happy while she skimmed a large percentage of the income Cole secured from his investors for herself. Apparently this isn't the first time she's done something like this. She's run similar scams in other parts of the world, which is how Interpol got involved."

"So why did she kill Cole?"

"I guess he noticed some discrepancies in the accounting and called her on it. She realized he'd become a liability and killed him. Anderson's role in the development didn't involve the financial side of things, so he had no idea what was going on."

"Is this Agent Baldini going to be okay?" Elva asked.

I nodded. "The bullet that went into her chest missed her major organs. Luke called 911 as soon as we were safely away and Agent Baldini was airlifted to the hospital."

"And Devlin and her partner?"

"In jail, thanks to Jason, who figured this all out days before I did and had been tracking her. She took off after I got away, but Jason had already planted a bug on her car."

"I guess all's well that ends well." Elva clasped her hands together. "Mary and Malia will be here any minute, so no more talk of murder."

Everyone agreed to a G-rated discussion while Cam and Kevin finished making the dinner we all planned to share and Carina and Kekoa chatted with Elva. Usually I loved the times when the condo family came together, but tonight I somehow felt empty inside. Not only had I failed to solve the murder before Jason, but my antics in Cole's room pretty much served as the final nail in the coffin that would prevent me from ever being a cop. I supposed that fact alone could account for my melancholy mood, but the truth of the matter was that I did feel bad about the way I'd treated Luke. Everyone was right; my problem was that my ego was bigger than my ability to carry it, and that usually ended up with my hurting the people I loved. Not that I loved Luke. Because I didn't. But you get what I mean.

"I think I'm going to take Sandy out for a walk."

"Dinner is almost ready," Sean reminded me.

"I know, but I'm not hungry. Catch you guys later."

No one tried to stop me, mostly I'm sure, because everyone knew where Sandy and I were really going. I did owe Luke an apology, and while I could certainly call him, somehow I knew this was one groveling that deserved to be delivered in person.

Besides, now that I knew Mr. B was really Agent Baldini, it made spending time with Sean and Kevin awkward. I'd stopped by the hospital to make certain for myself that she had survived, and she'd informed me that not only was she fine but she would be staying in the area for the time being. When I asked why she shared in strictest confidence that she was on the island not only to keep an eye on Devlin but to investigate Sean and Kevin for international smuggling.

I guess I could see how the men, as flight attendants, would be in a positon to smuggle goods between countries, but there was no way I was ever going to believe the men I'd grown to consider family would ever be involved in such a thing.

Still, I was sworn to secrecy, so I'd just have to bide my time and not do something stupid like blurt out what I knew until the investigation could be completed and my friends cleared of all suspicion.

I pulled up in front of Luke's house and turned off the car. Now that I was there I found my resolve was wavering. Sure, I owed Luke an apology, but did I really have the clarity of mind to offer it now? It really was fortunate that he'd been riding nearby on the day I unwisely decided to follow Helena Devlin. He'd just paused for a break and decided to check his messages when he heard the shot. He could simply have called 911 and let the authorities handle it, but instead he'd ridden toward the sound of the gunshot as fast as his horse would take him. Maybe I wasn't the only impulsive person in the relationship.

I decided, after several minutes of agonizing self-evaluation, that I needed to apologize, and there was no time like the present. I got out of the car, walked up to the front door with Sandy, and knocked.

"Lani?" Luke was genuinely surprised to find me standing on his stoop when he opened the door.

"I come bearing gifts." I held out a bag.

Luke took the bag and looked inside. "Cheetos?"

"That's all I could find on short notice. I'm really here to apologize." A damn tear rolled down my cheek. I hated it when my emotions betrayed me, but I was there to apologize, and apologize was what I was going to do. "You saved my life and I jumped down your throat. There really is no excuse for that except that I was scared, and I get overly cranky when I'm scared. I really am sorry. Can you ever forgive the way I've treated you these past few days?"

Luke didn't say anything right away. That made me nervous. Surely he'd forgive me. I don't know what I was going to do if he didn't.

"You're a complicated woman."

"I am."

"And you seem to have a tendency to get yourself into dicey situations."

"I do."

"But you don't like to be rescued?"

"I don't."

Luke stood silently, studying my face. It appeared he was trying to make up his mind about something. I just hoped I hadn't damaged our friendship beyond repair. Luke was someone I could count on, and I needed more friends like that in my life.

"You know that if we remain friends I'm going to continue to rescue you whether you want me to or not. I'm a Texan. Rescuing women in distress is part of the cowboy code."

"I know. And if you're the one to get into trouble I will likewise rescue you."

Luke smiled.

"So we're good?"

"We're good. I was thinking of going for a ride under the full moon. Would you like to join me?"

Hell no. I took a deep breath. "Sure. I'd love to."

Recipes

Recipes from Kathi
Banana Macadamia Nut Muffins
Loco Moco
Banana Cheese Pie
Supereasy Hawaiian Pie

Recipes submitted by readers
Hawaiian Breakfast Pizza
Pineapple Fritters with Mango Sauce
Irma Jersey's Pineapple Salad
Sea Foam Salad
Piña Colada Cake
I-45 Cake

Banana Macadamia Nut Muffins

1¼ cups mashed ripe bananas (about 3 large)
½ cup sugar
¼ cup dark brown sugar, firmly packed
½ cup (1 stick) butter, melted
¼ cup milk
1 large egg
1½ cups flour
1½ tsps. baking soda
¼ tsp. salt
½ tsp. ground nutmeg
½ tsp. cinnamon
2 cups macadamia nuts, toasted, chopped

Preheat oven to 350°F. Grease twelve muffin cups or line with muffin papers. Combine bananas, both sugars, butter, milk, and egg in large bowl. Mix in flour, baking soda, and spices. Fold in half of nuts. Divide batter among prepared muffin cups. Sprinkle tops of muffins with remaining macadamia nuts. Bake until muffins are golden brown and tester inserted into center comes out clean, about 25 minutes.

Loco Moco

A traditional loco moco:

Sticky rice
Hamburger patty
Eggs, any style
Brown gravy

This easy sausage variation makes 8 servings:

Minute rice (4 cups rice/4 cups water)
8 precooked sausage patties
8 eggs, any style (I scramble)

*Sausage gravy:
1 pkg. (16 oz.) ground sausage, browned
6 tbs. flour, shaken into 4 cups water

(I put water and flour into a plastic container with a lid and shake until flour is dissolved. Add to browned sausage. Simmer and stir until it thickens.)

Salt, pepper, and chili powder to taste

Place ⅛ rice on a plate. Layer on sausage patty over rice. Layer on 2 eggs. Cover with ⅛ sausage gravy.

(I sometimes garnish with chopped green onions.)

Banana Cheese Pie

2 large bananas
1 ready-made graham cracker crust (or make your own)
8 oz. cream cheese, softened
1 large box vanilla instant pudding
3 cups milk
1 small container Cool Whip
1 cup macadamia nuts, chopped

Slice bananas into pie crust. Mix cream cheese, pudding, and milk together and let set for 5 minutes. Pour over bananas in piecrust. Spread Cool Whip on top and garnish with macadamia nuts.

Supereasy Hawaiian Pie

1 can crushed pineapple, undrained (20 oz.)

1 box instant vanilla pudding mix (6 servings)

8 oz. sour cream

1 9-inch graham cracker crust

1 small container Cool Whip

I can sliced pineapple

8 maraschino cherries

½ cup flaked coconut

In a large bowl, combine crushed pineapple with its syrup, dry pudding mix, and sour cream. Mix until well combined. Spoon into pie crust. Frost with Cool Whip and decorate top with pineapple slices and cherries. Sprinkle with coconut.

Cover and chill at least 2 hours before serving.

Hawaiian Breakfast Pizza

Submitted by Joanne Kocourek

A special breakfast dish. My mom made something similar with Spam. I use lean ham as a healthy alternative. My children definitely prefer the dish made using ham and eliminating the olives.

1 8-oz. can refrigerated crescent roll dough
5 large eggs
¼ cup milk
¼ tsp. Italian seasoning
⅛ tsp. pepper
2 cups cubed ham, sautéed (or substitute one can cubed Spam)
¼ cup ripe tomato, diced
¼ cup sliced ripe olives (optional)
¼ cup mild onion, chopped
½ cup shredded Cheddar cheese
Heat oven to 375°F.

To make crust, unroll dough; separate into triangles. In cast-iron skillet or 12-inch deep dish pizza pan, place dough triangles with points toward center. Press together to cover bottom and ½ inch up side of skillet. Bake 10 minutes.

Meanwhile, in bowl, whisk together eggs, milk, Italian seasoning, and pepper; carefully pour mixture over crust. Bake 10 minutes or until egg mixture is almost set.

Sprinkle egg mixture with cubed ham (or cubed Spam Classic), tomato, olives, onion, and cheese. Bake 4 to 6 minutes or until cheese melts. Cut into wedges and enjoy.

Pineapple Fritters with Mango Sauce

Submitted by Taryn Lee

½ cup Panko (Japanese breadcrumbs)
¼ cup graham cracker crumbs
½ tsp. cinnamon
⅛ tsp. ginger
8 pineapple slices (fresh is best)
2 tbs. all-purpose flour
1 egg, beaten with 1 tbs. water
Vegetable oil for frying
Mango Sauce:
1 cup mango, sliced (fresh is best)
⅓ cup granulated sugar
1 tbs. lemon juice (fresh is best)

Puree mango for sauce. Pass through a sieve. Add sugar and lemon juice. Set aside.

Mix Panko, graham cracker crumbs, cinnamon, and ginger.
Dip the pineapple slices first intro the flour, then into the egg, and then into Panko.
Heat oil to 350 °F. Deep fry slices until golden brown.
Serve with mango sauce.

Note: You can sprinkle with sugar right out of the fryer for a touch more sweetness.

Irma Jersey's Pineapple Salad

Submitted by Connie Correll

A family holiday favorite from Cousin Irma.

1 large can pineapple
½ cup sugar
2 tbs. flour
2 eggs
Pinch of salt
2 oranges
24 (approx.) big marshmallows
1 cup whipping cream
1 cup slivered almonds

Drain juice from pineapple into a double boiler.
When hot, add sugar, flour, eggs, and salt. Cook until
thick and chill till cold. Cut pineapple, oranges, and
marshmallows into small, bite-size pieces. Whip
cream and add to the cold custard mixture. Pour over
fruit, add nuts, and let stand overnight.

Sea Foam Salad

Submitted by Vivian Shane

This salad has long been a tradition in my family, always served at Easter time for as long as I can remember. I have also made it for Christmas as a layered salad with red Jell-O as the bottom layer and Cool Whip on the top.

2 pkgs. lime Jell-O
2 cups hot water
2 small pkgs. (or I large) cream cheese
1 large can crushed pineapple juice
½ cup pecans
½ pt. whipping cream
2 tbs. sugar

Add Jell-O to hot water and stir until dissolved. Add cream cheese and beat with electric mixer. Let cool. Add pineapple, pecans, and whipping cream and sugar. Let set and serve.

Piña Colada Cake

Submitted by Della Williamson

Cake:
15-oz. can crushed pineapple in own juice, unsweetened
Yellow cake mix
2 eggs
1 tsp. rum flavoring extract.

Frosting:
3 cups confectioner's sugar (powdered sugar)
3 oz. cream cheese
1 tsp. vanilla
2 tbs. milk; add a little extra if needed for ease of spreading the frosting
Baker's Flaked Coconut

Place cream cheese in medium to large bowl; allow to come to room temperature. All ingredients should be room temperature. Drain the crushed pineapple and set aside for the cake.

Once well drained, measure juice to be sure it matches the amount of liquid required in the recipe. Instead of using the water or milk listed on the box for the cake, replace it with the pineapple juice. If needed, add extra milk, not water, to make the required amount. So just follow the recipe for the cake mix, exchanging the pineapple juice for the liquid listed on the box. Add 2 extra eggs. Most cake mixes call for oil; if so, change it to butter and double the amount. Melt it and allow it to cool a bit before mixing in. Mix in eggs one at a time. Add rum extract. Stir in the crushed pineapple.

Bake in a 9 x 13 pan according to directions on cake box. As stoves vary in temperature, test for doneness by inserting cool knife in center of cake. If it comes out clean, cake is done; if it doesn't, bake another 5 minutes and test with a clean knife; repeat if necessary. Cool completely.

Mix confectioner's sugar with cream cheese and vanilla. And 2 tbs. milk; add a teaspoon at a time if necessary to desired consistency for spreading. Frost cake. Cover with coconut.

I-45 Cake

Submitted by Pam Curran

Living in Texas, we have an I-45 highway, leading to the name of the recipe. This came from another teacher friend years ago. We always loved it when she brought it to school.

1 golden or yellow cake mix
1 egg
1 cup chopped pecans.

Mix well and press in a 9 x 13–inch pan.

1 8-oz. cream cheese, softened
2 eggs
⅔ cup coconut
⅔ cup chopped pecans

Mix the above ingredients and pour over cake. Bake in a 350 °F oven for 35 minutes until golden brown.

New Beginnings

Paradise Lake Cozy Mystery:

Pumpkins in Paradise
Snowmen in Paradise
Bikinis in Paradise
Christmas in Paradise
Puppies in Paradise
Halloween in Paradise

Tj Jensen Turtle Cove Mystery:

Barkley's Treasure – *April 2016*

Whales and Tails Cozy Mystery:

Romeow and Juliet
The Mad Catter
Grimm's Furry Tail
Much Ado About Felines
Legend of Tabby Hollow
Cat of Christmas Past
A Tale of Two Tabbies
The Great Catsby – *June 2016*

Seacliff High Mystery:

The Secret
The Curse
The Relic
The Conspiracy

The Grudge

Sand and Sea Hawaiian Mystery:
Murder at Dolphin Bay

Road to Christmas Romance:
Road to Christmas Past

Kathi Daley lives with her husband, kids, grandkids, and Bernese mountain dogs in beautiful Lake Tahoe. When she isn't writing, she likes to read (preferably at the beach or by the fire), cook (preferably something with chocolate or cheese), and garden (planting and planning, not weeding). She also enjoys spending time on the water when she's not hiking, biking, or snowshoeing the miles of desolate trails surrounding her home.

Kathi uses the mountain setting in which she lives, along with the animals (wild and domestic) that share her home, as inspiration for her cozy mysteries.

Kathi is a top 100 mystery writer for Amazon and she won the 2014 award for both *Best Cozy Mystery Author* and *Best Cozy Mystery Series*.

She currently writes five series: Zoe Donovan Cozy Mysteries, Whales and Tails Island Mysteries, Tj Jensen Southern Seashore Mysteries, Sand and Sea Hawaiian Mysteries, and Seacliff High Teen Mysteries.

Stay up to date with her newsletter, *The Daley Weekly*
http://eepurl.com/NRPDf

Kathi Daley Blog: publishes each Friday
http://kathidaleyblog.com

Webpage www.kathidaley.com

Facebook at Kathi Daley Books -
www.facebook.com/kathidaleybooks

Kathi Daley Teen –
www.facebook.com/kathidaleyteen

Kathi Daley Books Group Page –
https://www.facebook.com/groups/569578823146850/

E-mail - kathidaley@kathidaley.com

Goodreads:
https://www.goodreads.com/author/show/7278377.Kathi_Daley

Twitter at Kathi Daley@kathidaley -
https://twitter.com/kathidaley

Amazon Author Page -
https://www.amazon.com/author/kathidaley

BookBub -
https://www.bookbub.com/authors/kathi-daley

Pinterest -
http://www.pinterest.com/kathidaley/

Made in the USA
Monee, IL
24 January 2021

58562322R00125